"Sell Your Land To Me,"

Nathan said. "I'll give you a fair—a generous—
price. Then you can go home where you belong."

"No. I *will* succeed," Harriet informed him. "With
or without your help."

"I can sure as hell see why Hazards have been
feuding with Alistairs for a hundred years. You're as
stubborn as the rest of them were."

She whirled to confront him. "And I can see why
Alistairs chose to feud with Hazards," she retorted.
"How dare you sneak in under my guard and
pretend to help—"

"I wasn't pretending. I *did* help. Admit it!"

"Sure! So I'd be grateful. You only wanted to buy
my land right out from under me. You are the
lowest, meanest—"

He wasn't about to listen to insults. He pulled her
flush against him. She opened her mouth to lambaste
him again, and he shut her up the easiest way he
knew.

He covered her mouth with his....

Dear Reader,

Happy summertime reading from all of us here at Silhouette! As the days of summer wind to an end, take the time to curl up with August's wonderful love stories. These are books as hot as the most sizzling summer's day!

We start with Mary Lynn Baxter's *Man of the Month* novel *Tall in the Saddle,* which has a hero you'll never forget—Flint Carson, a man as rugged and untamed as the land he ranches. This is a book you'll want to read over and over again. It's a keeper!

Also in August comes a wild, witty romp from Lass Small, *The Molly Q.* Don't ask me to explain; I'll just say it has to do with computers, kidnapping and marvelous fun.

Rounding out August is *A Wolf in Sheep's Clothing,* a tie-in to July's *Never Tease a Wolf*—both by the talented Joan Johnston. And don't miss books from Naomi Horton, Ryanne Corey and Sally Goldenbaum. Each and every Silhouette Desire novel this month is one that I am keeping in my personal library.

So go wild with Desire—you'll be glad you did.

All the best,

Lucia Macro
Senior Editor

JOAN JOHNSTON

A WOLF IN SHEEP'S CLOTHING

SILHOUETTE *Desire*®

Published by Silhouette Books New York

America's Publisher of Contemporary Romance

SILHOUETTE BOOKS
300 East 42nd St., New York, N.Y. 10017

A WOLF IN SHEEP'S CLOTHING

ISBN: 0-373-05658-3

First Silhouette Books printing August 1991

Printed in the U.S.A.

Books by Joan Johnston

Silhouette Desire

Fit to Be Tied #424
Marriage by the Book #489
Never Tease a Wolf #652
A Wolf in Sheep's Clothing #658

JOAN JOHNSTON

became a closet reader of romances several years ago and started a habit of hiding one in her briefcase. Since then, she has published several historical novels as well as a number of contemporary romances. In addition to being an author, she is a lawyer, a teacher and the mother of two children. In her spare time, she enjoys sailing, horseback riding and camping.

ACKNOWLEDGMENTS

The Do's and Don't's for the Western Tenderfoot at the beginning of each chapter come from *The Greenhorn's Guide to the Woolly West* by Gwen Petersen, and are used with the permission of the author. I am also indebted to Gwen for the invaluable background information provided in her equally hilarious guide to ranch life, *The Ranch Woman's Manual.* Both books are available from Laffing Cow Press in Cheyenne, Wyoming.

I would also like to thank Jim Rolleri of the County Extension Service in Big Timber, Montana, for generously parting with every brochure on sheep ranching he could find in his files.

Finally, I would like to thank Jim Overstreet, a banker in Big Timber, Montana, who was kind enough to have lunch with me at The Grand and suggest the sorts of financial foibles to which a sheepman can be prone.

One

What do newcomers find abounding in Woolly West towns?
Answer: Quaintness and charm.

Nathan Hazard was mad enough to chew barbed wire. Cyrus Alistair was dead, but even in death the old curmudgeon had managed to thwart Nathan's attempts to buy his land. Cyrus had bequeathed his tiny Montana sheep ranch to a distant relative from Virginia, someone named Harry Alistair. For years that piece of property had been an itch Nathan couldn't scratch—a tiny scrap of Alistair land sitting square in the middle of the Hazard ranch—the last vestige of a hundred-year-old feud between the Hazards and the Alistairs.

Nathan had just learned from John Wilkinson, the executor of the Alistair estate, that Cyrus's heir hadn't let any grass grow under his feet. Harry Alistair had already arrived in the Boulder River Valley to take possession of Cyrus's ranch. Nathan only hoped the newest hard-nosed, ornery Alistair hadn't gotten too settled in. Because he wasn't staying. Not if Nathan had anything to say about it. Oh, he planned to offer a fair price. He was even willing to be generous if it came to that. But he was going to have that land.

Nathan gunned the engine on his pickup, disdaining the cavernous ruts in the dirt road that led to Cyrus's tiny, weather-beaten log cabin. It was a pretty good bet that once Harry Alistair got a look at the run-down condition of Cyrus's property, the Easterner would see the wisdom of selling. Cyrus's ranch—what there was of it—was falling down. There weren't more than five hundred sheep on the whole place.

Besides, what could a man from Williamsburg, Virginia, know about raising sheep? The greenhorn would probably take one look at the work, and risk, involved in trying to make a go of such a small, dilapidated spread and be glad to have Nathan take it off his hands. Nathan didn't contemplate what he would do if Harry Alistair refused to sell, because he simply wasn't going to take no for an answer.

As he drove up to the cabin, Nathan saw someone bounce up from one of the broken-down sheep pens that surrounded the barn. That had to be Harry Alistair. Nathan couldn't tell what the greenhorn was doing, but from the man's agitated movements it was plain something was wrong. A second later the fellow was racing for the barn. He came out another second later carrying a handful of supplies. Once again he ducked out of sight in the sheep pen.

Nathan sighed in disgust. The newcomer sure hadn't wasted any time getting himself into a pickle. For a moment Nathan considered turning his truck around and driving away. But despite the Hazard-Alistair feud, he couldn't leave without offering a helping hand. There were rules in the West that governed such conduct. A man in trouble wasn't friend or foe; he was merely a man in trouble. As such, he was entitled to whatever assistance Nathan could offer. Once the trouble was past and they were on equal footing again, Nathan could feel free to treat this Alistair as the mortal enemy the century-old feud made him.

Nathan slammed on the brakes and left his truck door hanging open as he raced across the snowy ground toward the sheep pen on foot. The closer Nathan got, the more his brow furrowed. The man had stood up again and put a hand behind his neck to rub the tension there. He was tall, but the body Nathan saw was gangly, the shoulders narrow. The man's face was smooth, unlined. Nathan hadn't been expecting someone so young and... the only word that came to mind was *delicate,* but he shied from thinking it. He watched the greenhorn drop out of sight again. With that graceful downward movement Nathan realized what had caused his confusion. That was no man in Cyrus Alistair's sheep pen—it was a woman!

When Nathan arrived at her side, he saw the problem right away. A sheep was birthing, but the lamb wasn't presenting correctly. The ewe was baaing in distress. The woman had dropped to her knees and was crooning to the animal in a low, raspy voice that sent shivers up Nathan's spine.

The woman was concentrating so hard on what she was doing that she wasn't even aware of Nathan until he asked, "Need some help?"

"What? Oh!" She looked up at him with stricken brown eyes. Her teeth were clenched on her lower lip and her cheeks were pale. He noticed her hand was trembling as she brushed her brown bangs out of her eyes with a slender forearm. "Yes. Please. I don't know what to do."

Nathan felt a constriction in his chest at the desperate note in her voice. He had an uncontrollable urge to protect her from the tragic reality she faced. The feeling was unfamiliar, and therefore uncomfortable. He ignored it as best he could, and quickly rolled up his sleeves. "Do you have some disinfectant handy?"

"Yes. Here." She poured disinfectant over his hands and arms.

Nathan shook off the excess and knelt beside the ewe. After a quick examination, he said flatly, "This lamb is dead."

"Oh, no! It's all my fault."

"Maybe not," Nathan contradicted. "Can't always save a case of dystocia."

"What?"

"The lamb is out of position. Its head is bent back, not forward along its legs like it ought to be."

"I read in a book what to do for a problem delivery. I just didn't realize…" She reached out a hand to briefly touch the lamb's foot that extended from the ewe. "Will the mother die, too?"

"Not if I can help it," Nathan said grimly. There was a long silence while he used soapy water to help the dead lamb slip free of the womb. Almost immediately contractions began again. "There's another lamb."

"Is it alive?" the woman asked, her voice full of hope.

"Don't know yet." Nathan wanted the lamb to be born alive more than he had wanted anything in a long time. Which made no sense at all. This was an Alistair sheep.

"Here it comes!" she exclaimed. "Is it all right?"

Nathan waited to see whether the lamb would suck air. When it didn't, he grabbed a nearby gunnysack and rubbed vigorously. The lamb responded by bleating pitifully. And Nathan let out the breath he hadn't known he'd been holding.

"It's alive!" she shouted.

"That it is," Nathan said with satisfaction. He cut the umbilical cord about an inch and a half from the lamb's navel and asked, "Where's the iodine?"

Nathan helped the ewe to her feet while the woman ran to fetch a wide-mouth jar full of iodine. When she returned he held the lamb up by its front legs and sloshed the jar over the navel cord until it was covered with iodine. He set the lamb back down beside its mother where, after some bumping and searching with its nose, it found a teat and began to nurse.

Nathan glanced at the woman to share the moment, which he found profoundly moving no matter how many times he'd seen it. Once he did, he couldn't take his eyes off her.

She was watching the nursing lamb, and her whole face reflected a kind of joy he had seldom seen and wasn't sure he had ever felt. When the lamb made a loud, slurping sound, a laugh of relief bubbled up from her throat. And she looked up into his eyes and smiled.

He was stunned. Poleaxed. Smitten. In a long-ago time he would have thrown her on his horse and ridden off into the sunset. But this was now, and he was a civilized man. So he simply swallowed hard, gritted his teeth and smiled back.

Her smile revealed a slight space between her front teeth that made her look almost winsome. A dimple appeared in her left cheek when the smile became a grin. Her bangs had fallen back over her brows, and it took all his willpower to leave it alone. Her nose was small and tilted up at the end, and he noticed her cheeks, now that they weren't so pale, were covered with a scattering of freckles. Her lips were full, despite the wide smile, and her chin, tilted up toward him, seemed to ask for his touch. He had actually lifted a hand toward her when he realized what he was about to do.

Nathan was confused by the strength of his attraction to the woman. He didn't need—refused to take on—any more obligations in his lifetime. This was a woman who looked in great need of a lot of care and attention. This kind of woman spelled RESPONSIBILITY in capital letters. He shrugged inwardly. He had done his share of taking care of the helpless. He hadn't begrudged the sacrifice, because it had been necessary, but he was definitely gun-shy. When he chose a woman to share his life, it would be someone who could stand on her own two feet, someone who could be a helpmate and an equal partner. He would never choose someone like the winsome woman kneeling before him, whose glowing brown eyes beseeched him to take her into his arms and comfort her there.

Not by a long shot!

Nathan bolted to his feet, abruptly ending the intense feeling of closeness he felt with the woman. "Where the hell is Harry Alistair?" he demanded in a curt voice. "And what the hell are you doing out here trying to handle a complicated lambing all alone?"

His stomach knotted when he saw the hurt look in her eyes at his abrupt tone of voice, but he didn't have a chance even to think about apologizing before a spark of defiance lit up her beautiful brown eyes, and she rose to her feet. Her hands balled into fists and found her hipbones. She was tall. Really tall. He stood six foot three and she was staring him practically in the eye.

"You're looking for Harry Alistair?" she asked in a deceptively calm voice.

"I am."

"What for?"

"That's between him and me. Look, do you know where he is or not?"

"I do."

But that was all she said. Nathan was damned if he was going to play games with her. He yanked the worn Stetson off his head, forked an agitated hand through his blond hair and settled the cowboy hat back in place over his brow. He placed his fists on his hips in a powerful masculine version of her pose and grated out, "Well, where the hell is he?"

"*He's* standing right here."

There was a long pause while Nathan registered what she'd said. "*You're* Harry Alistair?"

"Actually, my name is Harriet." She forgave him for his rudeness with one of those engaging smiles and said, "But my friends all call me Harry."

She stuck out her hand for him to shake, and before he could curb his automatic reaction he had her hand clasped in his. It was soft. Too damn soft for a woman who hoped to survive the hard life of a Montana sheep rancher. He held on to her hand as he examined her—the Harry Alistair he had come to see—more closely.

He was looking for reasons to find fault with her, to prove he couldn't possibly be physically attracted to her, and he found them. She was dressed in a really god-awful outfit: brand-new bibbed overalls, a red-and-black plaid wool shirt, a down vest, galoshes for heaven's sake, and a Harley's Feed Store baseball cap, which meant she'd already been to Slim Harley's Feed Store in Big Timber. Nathan hadn't realized her hair was so long, but two childish braids fell over each shoulder practically to her breasts.

Nothing wrong with them, a voice inside taunted.

Nathan forced his eyes back up to her face, which now bore an expression of amusement. A slow red flush crept up his neck. There was no way he could hide it or stop it. His Swedish ancestors had bequeathed him blue eyes and blond hair and skin that got ruddy in the sun, but never tanned. Unfortunately his Nordic complexion also displayed his feelings when he most wanted them hidden. He suddenly dropped her hand as though it had caught fire.

"We have to talk," he said flatly.

"I'd like that," Harry replied. "After everything we've just been through together, I feel like we're old friends, Mr.— Oh, my," she said with a self-deprecating laugh. "I don't even know your name."

"Nathan Hazard."

"Come on inside, Nathan Hazard, and have a cup of coffee, and we'll talk."

Nathan was pretty sure he could conduct his business right here. After all, how many words did it take to say "I want to buy this place"? Only six. But he was curious to see the inside of Cyrus Alistair's place. He had heard the tiny log cabin called "rustic" by those who had actually been inside, though they were few and far between.

Against his better judgment Nathan said, "Sure. A cup of coffee sounds good."

"I don't have things very organized," Harry apologized.

Nathan soon realized that was an understatement. Harry took him in through the back door, which led to the kitchen. What he saw was *chaos*. What he felt was *disappointment*. Because despite everything he had already seen of her, he had been holding out hope that he was wrong about Harry Alistair. The shambles he beheld in the kitchen of the tiny cabin—dishes piled high in the sink, half-empty bottles of formula on the counters, uneaten meals side by side with stacks of brochures on the table, several bags of garbage in one corner, and a lamb sleeping on a wadded-up blanket in the other—confirmed his worst fears. Harry Alistair needed a caretaker. This wasn't a woman who was ever going to be anyone's equal partner.

Harry had kicked off her galoshes when she came in the door, and let them lie where they fell. Her down vest warmed the back of the kitchen chair, and she hooked her Harley's Feed Store cap on a deer antler that graced the dingy, wooden-planked wall.

Poor woman, he thought. She must have given up trying to deal with all the mess and clutter. He hardened himself against feeling sympathy for her. He was more convinced than ever that he would be doing her a favor by buying Cyrus's place from her.

While he stood staring, Harry grabbed some pottery mugs for the coffee from kitchen cupboards that appeared to be all but bare. He was able to notice that because all the cupboards hung open on dragging hinges. As quickly as she shoved the painted yellow kitchen cupboards closed, they sprang open again. And stayed that way. She turned to him, shrugged and let go with another one of her smiles. He stuck his hands deep into his pockets to keep from reaching out to enfold her in his arms.

Not the woman for me, he said to himself.

The walls and floor of the room consisted of unfinished wooden planks. A step down from "rustic," he thought. More like "primitive." The refrigerator was so old that the top was rounded instead of square. The gas stove was equally ancient, and she had to light the burner with a match.

"Darned thing doesn't work from the pilot," Harry explained as she set a dented metal coffeepot on the burner. "Make yourself at home," she urged, seating herself at the kitchen table.

Nathan set his Stetson on the table and draped his sheepskin coat over the back of one of the three chrome-legged chairs at the Formica table. Then he flattened the torn plastic seat and sat down. The table was cluttered with brochures. One title leaped out at him—"Sheep Raising for Beginners." He didn't have a chance to comment on it before she started talking.

"I'm from Williamsburg, Virginia," she volunteered. "I didn't even know my Great-Uncle Cyrus. It was really a surprise when Mr. Wilkinson from the bank contacted me. At first I couldn't believe it. Me, inheriting a sheep ranch! I suppose the sensible thing would have been to let Mr. Wilkinson sell the place for me. He said there was a buyer anxious to have it. Then I thought about what it would be like to have a place of my very own, far away from—" She jumped up and crossed to the stove to check the coffeepot.

Nathan wanted her to finish that sentence. What, or whom, had she wanted to escape? What, or who, had made her unhappy enough that she had to run all the way to Montana? He fought down the possessive, protective feelings that arose. She didn't belong to him. Never would.

She was talking in breathless, jerky sentences, which was how he knew she was nervous. It was as though she wasn't used to entertaining a man in her kitchen. Maybe she wasn't. He wished he knew for sure.

Not your kind of woman, he repeated to himself.

"Do you have a place around here?" Harry asked.

Nathan cleared his throat and said with a rueful smile, "You could say I have a place that goes all around here."

He watched her brows lower in confusion at his comment. She filled the two coffee mugs to the very brim and brought them carefully to the table.

"Am I supposed to know what that means?" she asked as she seated herself across from him again.

"My sheep ranch surrounds yours." When she still looked confused he continued, "Your property sits square in the center of mine. Your access road to the highway runs straight across my land."

A brilliant smile lit her face, and she cocked her head like a brown sparrow on a budding limb and quipped, "Then we most certainly *are* neighbors, aren't we? I'm so glad you came to see me, Nathan—is it all right if I call you Nathan?—so we can get to know each other. I could really use some advice. You see—"

"Wait a minute," he interrupted.

In the first place it wasn't all right with him if she called him Nathan. It would be much more difficult to be firm with her if they were on a first-name basis. In the second place he hadn't come here to be neighborly; he had come to make an offer on her land. And in the third, and most important, place, he had *absolutely no intention of offering her any advice.* And he was going to tell her all those things . . . just as soon as she stopped smiling so trustingly at him.

"Look, Harry-et," he said, pausing a second between the two syllables, unable to make himself address her by the male nickname. "You probably should have taken the banker's advice. If the rest of this cabin looks as bad as the kitchen, it can't be very comfortable. The buildings and sheds are a disgrace. Your hay fields are fallow. Your access road is a mass of ruts. You'll be lucky to make ends meet let alone earn enough from this sheep ranch you inherited to enjoy any kind of pleasant life. The best advice I can give you is to sell this place to me and go back to Virginia where you belong.''

He watched her full lips firm into a flat line and her jaw tauten. Her chin came up pugnaciously. ''I'm not selling out.''

''Why the hell not?'' he retorted in exasperation.

''Because.''

He waited for her to explain. But she was keeping her secrets to herself. He was convinced now that she must be running from something . . . or someone.

''I'm going to make a go of this place. I can do it. I may not be experienced, but I'm intelligent and hard-working and I have all the literature on raising sheep that I could find.''

Nathan stuck the brochure called ''Sheep Raising for Beginners'' under her nose and said, ''None of these brochures will compensate for practical experience. Look what happened this afternoon. What would you have done if I hadn't come along?'' He had the unpleasant experience of watching her chin drop to her chest and her cheeks flush while her thumb brushed anxiously against the plain pottery mug.

''I would probably have lost both lambs, and the ewe, as well,'' she admitted in a low voice. She looked up at him, her brown eyes liquid with tears she was trying to blink away. "I owe you my thanks. I don't know how I can ever repay you. I know I have a lot to learn. But—" she leaned forward, and her voice became urgent "—I intend to work as hard as I have to, night and day if necessary, until I succeed!"

Nathan was angry and irritated. She wasn't going to succeed; she was going to fail miserably. And unless he could somehow talk her into selling this place to him, he was going to have to stand by and watch it happen. Because he *absolutely, positively,* was *not* going to offer to help. There were no ifs, ands or buts about it. He had been through this before. A small commitment had a way of mushrooming out of control. Start cutting pines and pretty soon you had a whole mountain meadow.

"Look, Harry-et," he said, "the reason I came here today is to offer to buy this place from you."

"It's not for sale."

Nathan sighed. She'd said it as if she'd meant it. He had no choice except to try to convince her to change her mind. "Sheep ranching involves a whole lot more than lambing and shearing, Harry-et." He was distracted from his train of thought by the way the flush on her cheeks made her freckles show up. He forced his attention back where it belonged and continued. "For instance, do you have any idea what wool pool you're in?"

She raised a blank face and stared at him.

"Do you even know what a wool pool is?"

She shook her head.

"A wool pool enables small sheepmen like yourself to concentrate small clips of wool into carload lots so that they can get a better price on—" He cut himself off. He was supposed to be proving her ignorance to her, not educating it away. He ignored her increasingly distressed look and asked, "Do you have any idea what's involved with docking and castrating lambs?"

This time she nodded, but the flush on her face deepened.

"What about keeping records? Do you have any accounting experience?"

"A little," she admitted in a quiet voice.

He felt like a desperado in a black hat threatening the schoolmarm, but he told himself it was for her own good in the long run and continued, "Can you figure adjusted weaning weight ratios? Measure ram performance? Calculate shearing dates? Compute feed gain ratios?"

By now she was violently shaking her head. A shiny tear streaked one cheek.

He pushed himself up out of his chair. He braced one callused palm on the table and leaned across to cup her jaw in his other hand and lift her chin. He looked into her eyes, and it took every bit of determination he had not to succumb to the plea he saw there. "I can't teach you to run this ranch. I have a business of my own that needs tending. You can't make it on your own, Harry-et. Sell your land to me."

"No."

"I'll give you a fair—a generous—price. Then you can go home where you belong."

She was out of his grasp and gone before he had time to stop her. She didn't go far, just to the sink, where she stood in front of the stack of dirty dishes and stared out the dirt-clouded window at the ramshackle sheep pens and the derelict barn. "I will succeed. With or without your help."

She sounded so sure of herself, despite the fact that she was doomed to fail. Nathan refused to admire her. He chose to be furious with her instead. In three angry strides he was beside her. "You're as stubborn as every other hard-nosed, ornery Alistair who ever lived on this land!" He snorted in disgust. "I can sure as hell see now why Hazards have been feuding with Alistairs for a hundred years."

She whirled to confront him. "And I can see why Alistairs chose to feud with Hazards," she retorted. "How dare you pretend to be a friend!" She poked him in the chest with a stiff finger. "How dare you sneak in under my guard and pretend to help—"

"I wasn't pretending," he said heatedly, grabbing her wrist to keep her from poking him again. "I *did* help. Admit it!"

"Sure! So I'd be grateful. All the time you only wanted to buy my land right out from under me. You are the lowest, meanest—"

He wasn't about to listen to any insults from a greenhorn female! A moment later her arm was twisted up behind her and he had pulled her flush against him. She opened her mouth to lambaste him again and he shut her up the quickest, easiest way he knew. He covered her mouth with his.

Nathan was angry, and he wasn't gentle. That is, until he felt her lips soften under his. It felt like he had been wanting her for a long time. His mouth moved slowly over hers while his hand cupped her head and kept her still so he could take what he needed. She struggled against his hold, her breasts brushing against his chest, her hips hard against his. That only made him want her more. It was when he felt her trembling that he came to his senses, mortified at the uncivilized way he had treated her.

He abruptly released the hand he had twisted behind her back. But instead of coming up to slap him, as he had expected, her palm reached up to caress his cheek. Her fingertips followed the shape of his cheekbone upward to his temple, where she threaded her fingers into his hair and slowly pulled his head back down. And then she kissed him back.

That was when he realized she was trembling with desire. Not fear. Desire. With both hands free he cupped her buttocks and pulled her hard against him. For every thrust he made, she countered. He was as full and hard as he had ever been in his life. His tongue ravaged her mouth, and she responded with an ardor that made him hungry for her. He spread urgent kisses across her face and neck, but they didn't satisfy as much as the taste of her, so he sought her mouth again. His tongue found the space between her teeth. And the inside of her lip. And the roof of her mouth. When he mimicked the thrust and parry of lovers, she held his tongue and sucked it until he thought his head was going to explode.

When he slipped his hand over her buttocks and between her legs, she moaned, a sound that came from deep in her throat and spoke of an agony of unappeased passion.

And the lamb in the corner bleated.

Nathan lifted his head and stared at the woman in his arms. Her brown eyes were half-veiled by her lids, and her pupils were dilated. She was breathing as heavily as he was, her lips parted to gasp air. Her knees had already buckled, and his grasp on her was all that kept them both from the floor.

Are you out of your mind?

He tried to step away, but her hand still clutched his hair. He reached up and drew her hand away. She suddenly seemed to realize he had changed his mind and backed up abruptly. Nathan refused to look at her face. He already felt bad enough. He had come within a lamb's tail of making love to Harry-et Alistair. He had made a narrow escape, for which he knew he would later, when his body wasn't so painfully objecting, be glad for.

"I think it's time you left, Mr. Hazard," Harry said in a rigidly controlled voice.

He couldn't leave without trying once more to accomplish what he'd come to do. "Are you sure you won't—"

The change in her demeanor was so sudden that it took him by surprise. Her expression was fierce, determined. "I will not sell this land," she said through clenched teeth. "Now get out of here before—"

"Goodbye, Harry-et. If you have a change of heart, John Wilkinson at the bank knows how to get in touch with me."

He settled his hat on his head and pulled it down with a tug. Then he shrugged broad shoulders into his sheepskin-lined coat. Before he was even out the kitchen door Harry Alistair had already started heating a bottle of formula for the lamb she had snuggled in her arms. It was the first time he'd ever envied one of the fleecy orphans.

The last thing Nathan Hazard wanted to do was leave that room. But he turned resolutely and marched out the door. As he gunned the engine of his truck, he admitted his encounter with Harry-et Alistair had been a very close call.

Not the woman for you, he reminded himself. *Definitely not the woman for you.*

TWO

Are there bachelors in them thar hills?
Answer: Yep.

Once the lamb had been fed and settled back on its pallet, Harry sank into a kitchen chair, put her elbows on the table and let her head drop into her hands. What on earth had she been thinking to let Nathan Hazard kiss her like that! And worse, why had she kissed him back in such a wanton manner? It was perfectly clear now that she hadn't been *thinking* at all; she had been feeling, and the feelings had been so overwhelming that they hadn't allowed for any kind of rational consideration.

Harry had felt an affinity to the rancher from the instant she'd laid eyes on him. His broad shoulders, his narrow hips, the dusting of fine blond hair on his powerful forearms all appealed to her. His eyes were framed by crow's-feet that gave character to a sharp-boned, perfectly chiseled face. That pair of sapphire-blue eyes, alternately curious and concerned, had stolen her heart.

Harry wasn't surprised that she was attracted to someone more handsome than any man had a right to be. What amazed her was that having known Nathan Hazard for only a matter of hours she would readily have trusted him with her life. That simply wasn't logical. Although, Harry supposed in retrospect, she had probably seen in Nathan Hazard exactly what she wanted to see. She had needed a legendary, bigger-than-life western hero, someone tall, rugged and handsome to come along and rescue her. And he had obligingly arrived.

And he had been stunning in his splendor, though that had consisted merely of a pair of butter-soft jeans molded to his long legs, western boots, a dark blue wool shirt topped by a sheepskin-lined denim jacket, and a Stetson he had pulled down so that it left his features shadowed. The shaggy, silver-blond hair that fell a full inch over his collar had made him look un-tamed, perhaps untamable. Harry remembered won-dering what such fine blond hair might feel like to touch. His lower lip was full, and he had a wide, easy smile that pulled one side of his mouth up a little higher than the other. She had also wondered, she re-alized with chagrin, what it would be like to kiss that mouth. Unbelievably she had actually indulged her fantasies.

Harry wasn't promiscuous. She wasn't even sexually experienced when it came right down to it. So she had absolutely no explanation for what had just happened between her and the Montana sheepman. She only knew she had felt an urgent, uncontrollable need to touch Nathan Hazard, to kiss him and to have him kiss her back. And she hadn't wanted him to stop there. She had wanted him inside her, mated to her.

Her mother and father, not to mention her brother, Charlie, and her eight uncles and their dignified, decorous wives, would have been appalled to think that any Williamsburg Alistair could have behaved in such a provocative manner with a man she had only just met. Harry was a little appalled herself.

But then nothing in Montana was going the way she had planned.

It had seemed like such a good idea, when she had gotten the letter from John Wilkinson, to come to the Boulder River Valley and learn how to run Great-Uncle Cyrus's sheep ranch. She loved animals and she loved being out-of-doors and she loved the mountains—she had heard that southwestern Montana had a lot of beautiful mountains. She had expected opposition to such a move from her family, so she had carefully chosen the moment to let them know about her decision.

No Alistair ever argued at the dinner table. So, sitting at the elegant antique table that had been handed down from Alistair to Alistair for generations, she had waited patiently for a break in the dinner conversation and calmly announced, "I've decided to take advantage of my inheritance from Great-Uncle Cyrus. I'll be leaving for Montana at the end of the week."

"But you can't possibly manage a sheep ranch on your own, Harriet," her mother admonished in a cultured voice. "And since you're bound to fail, darling, I can't understand why you would even want to give it a try. Besides," she added, "think of the smell!"

Harry—her mother cringed every time she heard the masculine nickname—had turned her compelling brown eyes to her father, looking for an encouraging word.

"Your mother is right, sweetheart," Terence Waverly Alistair said. "My daughter, a sheep farmer?" His thick white brows lowered until they nearly met at the bridge of his nose. "I'm afraid I can't lend my support to such a move. You haven't succeeded at a single job I've found for you, sweetheart. Not the one as a teller in my bank, not the one as a secretary, nor the the one as a medical receptionist. You've gotten yourself fired for ineptness at every single one. It's foolhardy to go so far—Montana is a long way from Virginia, my dear—merely to fail yet again. Besides," he added, "think of the cold!"

Harry turned her solemn gaze toward her older brother, Charles. He had been her champion in the past. He had even unbent so far as to call her Harry when their parents weren't around. Now she needed his support. Wanted his support. Begged with her eyes for his support.

"I'm afraid I have to agree with Mom and Dad, Harriet."

"But, Charles—"

"Let me finish," he said in a determined voice. Harry met her brother's sympathetic gaze as he continued. "You're only setting yourself up for disappointment. You'll be a lot happier if you learn to accept your limitations."

"Meaning?" Harry managed to whisper past the ache in her throat.

"Meaning you just aren't clever enough to pull it off, Harriet. Besides," he added, "think of all that manual labor!"

Harry felt the weight of a lifetime of previous failures in every concerned but discouraging word her family had offered. They didn't believe she could do it. She took a deep breath and let it out. She could hardly blame them for their opinion of her. To be perfectly honest, she had never given them any reason to think otherwise. So why was she so certain that this time things would be different? Why was she so certain that this time she would succeed? Because she knew something they didn't: *she had done all that failing in the past on purpose!*

Harry was paying now for years of deception. It had started innocently enough when she was a child and her mother had wanted her to take ballet lessons. At six Harry had already towered over her friends. Gawky and gangly, she knew she was never going to make a graceful prima ballerina. One look at her mother's face, however, and Harry had known she couldn't say, "No, thank you. I'd rather be playing basketball."

Instead, she had simply acquired two left feet. It had worked. Her ballet instructor had quickly labeled her irretrievably clumsy and advised Isabella Alistair that she would only be throwing her money away if Harriet continued in the class. Isabella was forced to admit defeat. Thus, unbeknownst to her parents, Harry had discovered at a very early age a passive way of resisting them.

Over the years Harry had never said no to her parents. It had been easier simply to go along with whatever they had planned. Piano lessons were thwarted with a deaf ear; embroidery had been abandoned as too bloody; and her brief attempt at tennis had resulted in a broken leg.

As she had gotten older, the stakes had gotten higher. She had only barely avoided a plan to send her away to college at Radcliffe by getting entrance exam scores so low that they had astonished the teachers who had watched her get straight A's through high school. She had been elated when her distraught parents had allowed her to enroll at the same local university her friends from high school were attending.

Harry knew she should have made some overt effort to resist each time her father had gotten her one of those awful jobs after graduation, simply stood up to him and said, ''No, I'd rather be pursuing a career that I've chosen for myself.'' But old habits were hard to break. It had been easier to prove inept at each and every one.

When her parents chose a husband for her, she had resorted to even more drastic measures. She had concealed what looks she had, made a point of reciting her flaws to her suitor and resisted his amorous advances like a starched-up prude. She had led the young man to contemplate life with a plain, clumsy, cold-natured, brown-eyed, brown-haired, freckle-faced failure. He had beat a hasty retreat.

Now a lifetime of purposeful failure had come home to roost. She couldn't very well convince her parents she was ready to let go of the apron strings when she had so carefully convinced them of her inability to succeed at a single thing they had set for her to do. She might have tried to explain to them her failure had only been a childish game that had been carried on too long, but that would mean admitting she had spent her entire life deceiving them. She couldn't bear to hurt them like that. Anyway, she didn't think they would believe her if she told them her whole inept life had been a sham.

Now Harry could see, with the clarity of twenty-twenty hindsight, that she had hurt herself even more than her parents by the choices she had made. But the method of dealing with her parents' manipulation, which she had started as a child and continued as a teenager, she had found impossible to reverse as an adult. Until now. At twenty-six she finally had the perfect opportunity to break the pattern of failure she had pursued for a lifetime. She only hoped she hadn't waited too long.

Harry was certain she could manage her Great-Uncle Cyrus's sheep ranch. She was certain she could do anything she set her brilliant mind to do. After all, it had taken brilliance to fail as magnificently, and selectively, as she had all these years. So now, when she was determined to succeed at last, she had wanted her family's support. It was clear she wasn't going to get it. And she could hardly blame them for it. She was merely reaping what she had so carefully sowed.

Harry had a momentary qualm when she wondered whether they might be right. Maybe she was biting off more than she could chew. After all, what did she know about sheep or sheep ranching? Then her chin tilted up and she clenched her hands in her lap under the table. They were wrong. She wouldn't fail. She could learn what she didn't know. And she would succeed.

Harriet Elizabeth Alistair was convinced in her heart that she wasn't a failure. Surely, once she made up her mind to stop failing, she could. Once she was doing something she had chosen for herself, she was bound to succeed. She would show them all. She wasn't what they thought her—someone who had to be watched and protected from herself and the cold, cruel world around her. Rather, she was a woman with hopes and dreams, none of which she had been allowed—or rather, allowed herself—to pursue.

Like a pioneer of old, Harry wanted to go west to build a new life. She was prepared for hard work, for frigid winter mornings and searing summer days. She welcomed the opportunity to build her fortune with the sweat of her brow and the labor of her back. Harry couldn't expect her family to understand why she wanted to try to make it on her own in a cold, smelly, faraway place where she would have to indulge in manual labor. She had something to prove to herself. This venture was the Boston Tea Party and the Alamo and Custer's Last Stand all rolled into one. In the short run she might lose a few battles, but she was determined to win the war.

At last Harry broke the awesome silence that had descended on the dinner table. "Nothing you've said has changed my mind," she told her family. "I'll be leaving at the end of the week."

Nothing her family said the following week, and they had said quite a lot, had dissuaded Harry from the course she had set for herself. She had been delighted to find, when she arrived a week later in Big Timber, the town closest to Great-Uncle Cyrus's ranch, that at least she hadn't been deceived about the beauty of the mountains in southwestern Montana. The Crazy Mountains provided a striking vista to the north, while the majestic, snow-capped Absarokas greeted her to the south each morning. But they were the only redeeming feature in an otherwise daunting locale.

The Boulder River Valley was a desolate place in late February. The cottonwoods that lined the Boulder River, which meandered the length of the valley, were stripped bare of leaves. And the grass, what wasn't covered by patches of drifted snow, was a ghastly straw-yellow. All that might have been bearable if only she hadn't found such utter decay when she arrived at Great-Uncle Cyrus's ranch.

Her first look at the property she had inherited had been quite a shock. Harry had been tempted to turn tail and run back to Williamsburg. But something— perhaps the beauty of the mountains, but more likely the thought of facing her family if she gave up without even trying—had kept her from giving John Wilkinson the word to sell. She would never go home until she could do so with her head held high, the owner and manager of a prosperous sheep ranch.

Harry had discovered dozens of reasons to question her decision ever since she had moved to Montana, not the least of which was the meeting today with her nearest neighbor. Nathan Hazard hadn't exactly fulfilled her expectations of the typical western hero. A more provoking, irritating, exasperating man she had never known! Whether he admitted it or not, it had been a pretty sneaky thing to do, helping her so generously with the difficult lambing when he knew all along he was only softening her up so that he could make an offer on her land.

Thoughts of the difficult birthing reminded her that she still had to dispose of the dead lamb. Harry knew she ought to bury it, but the ground was frozen. She couldn't imagine burning it. And she couldn't bear the thought of taking the poor dead lamb somewhere up into the foothills and leaving it among the juniper and jack pine for nature's scavengers to find. None of the brochures she had read discussed this particular problem. Harry knew there must be some procedures the local ranchers followed. Surely they also had deaths at lambing time. But she would dig a hole in the frozen ground with her fingernails before she asked Nathan Hazard what to do.

For now Harry decided to move the dead lamb behind the barn and cover it with a tarp. As long as the weather stayed cold, the body wouldn't decay. When she could spare the time, she would take a trip into Big Timber and strike up a conversation with Slim Harley at the feed store. Somehow she would casually bring up the subject of dead lambs in the conversation and get the answers she needed. Harry's lips twisted wryly. Western conversations certainly tended to have a grittier tone than those in the East.

Harry couldn't put off what had to be done. She slipped her vest back on, pulled her cap down on her head and stepped back into her galoshes. A quick search turned up some leather work gloves in the drawer beside the sink. A minute later she was headed back out to the sheep pens.

Harry actually shuddered when she picked up the dead lamb. It had stiffened in death. It was also heavier than she had expected, so she had to hold it close to her chest in order to carry it. Despite everything Harry had read about not getting emotionally involved, she was unable to keep from mourning the animal's death. It seemed like such a waste. Although, if the lamb had lived it would have gone to market, where it would eventually have become lamb chops on some eastern dinner table.

Maybe she ought to call Nathan Hazard and take him up on his offer, after all.

Before Harry had a chance to indulge her bout of maudlin conjecture she heard another sheep baaing in distress.

Not again!

Harry raced for the sheep pens where she had separated the ewes that were ready to deliver. Instead she discovered a sheep had already given birth to one lamb; while she watched it birthed a twin. Harry had learned from her extensive reading that her sheep had been genetically bred so that they bore twins, thus doubling the lamb crop. But to her it was a unique happening. She stopped and leaned against the pen and smiled with joy at having witnessed such a miraculous event.

Then she realized she had work to do. The cords had to be cut and dipped in iodine. And the ewe and her lambs had to be moved into a jug, a small pen separate from the other sheep, for two or three days until the lambs had bonded with their mothers and gotten a little stronger.

Harry had read that lambing required constant attention from a rancher, but she hadn't understood that to mean she would get no sleep, no respite. For the rest of the night she never had a chance to leave the sheep barn, as the ewes dropped twin lambs that lived and died depending on the whims of fate. The stack under the tarp beside her barn got higher. If Harry had found a spare second, she would have swallowed her pride and called Nathan Hazard for help. But by the time she got a break near dawn, the worst seemed to be over. Harry had stood midwife to the delivery of forty-seven lambs. Forty-three were still alive.

She dragged herself into the house, and only then realized she had forgotten about the orphan lamb in her kitchen. He was bleating pitifully from hunger. Despite her fatigue, Harry took the time to fix the lamb a bottle. She fell asleep sitting on the wooden-plank floor with her back against the wooden-plank wall, with the hungry lamb in her lap sucking at a nippled Coke bottle full of milk replacer.

That was how Nathan Hazard found her the following morning at dawn.

Nathan had lambing of his own going on, but unlike Harriet Alistair, he had several hired hands to help with the work. When suppertime arrived, he left the sheep barn and came inside to a hot meal that Katoya, the old Blackfoot Indian woman who was his housekeeper, had ready and waiting for him.

Katoya had mysteriously arrived on the Hazard doorstep on the day Nathan's mother had died, as though by some prearranged promise, to take her place in the household. Nathan had been sixteen at the time. No explanation had ever been forthcoming as to why the Blackfoot woman had come. And despite Nathan's efforts in later years to ease the older woman's chores, Katoya still worked every day from dawn to dusk with apparent tirelessness, making Nathan's house a home.

As Nathan sat down at the kitchen table, he wondered whether Harriet Alistair had found anything worth eating in her bare cupboards. The fact he should find himself worrying about an Alistair, even if it was a woman, made him frown.

"Were you able to buy the land?" Katoya asked as she poured coffee into his cup.

Nathan had learned better than to try to keep secrets from the old Indian woman. "Harry Alistair wouldn't sell," he admitted brusquely.

The diminutive Blackfoot woman merely nodded. "And so the feud will go on." She seated herself in a rocker in the kitchen that was positioned to get the most heat from the old-fashioned wood stove.

Nathan grimaced. "Yeah."

"Is it so important to own the land?"

Nathan turned to face her and saw skin stretched tight with age over high, wide cheekbones, and black hair threaded with silver in two braids over her shoulders. He suddenly wondered how old she was. Certainly she had clung to the old Blackfoot ways. "It must be the Indian in you," he said at last, "that doesn't feel the same need as I do to possess land."

Katoya looked back at him with eyes that were a deep black well of wisdom. "The Indian knows what the white man has never learned. You cannot own the land. You can only use it for so long as you walk the earth."

Katoya started the rocker moving, and its creak made a familiar, comforting sound as Nathan ate the hot lamb stew she had prepared for him.

Nathan had to admit there was a lot to be said for the old woman's argument. Why was he so determined to own that piece of Alistair land? After all, when he was gone, who would know or care? Maybe he could have accepted Katoya's point of view if he hadn't met Harry Alistair first. Now he couldn't leave things the way they stood. That piece of land smack in the middle of his spread had always been a burr under the saddle. He didn't intend to stop bucking until the situation was remedied.

Nathan refilled his own coffee cup to keep the old woman from having to get up again, then settled down into the kitchen chair with his legs stretched out toward the stove. Because he respected Katoya's advice, Nathan found himself explaining the situation. "The Harry Alistair who inherited the land from Cyrus turned out to be a woman, Harry-et Alistair. She's greener than buffalo grass in spring and doesn't know a thing about sheep that hasn't come out of an extension service bulletin. Harry-et Alistair hasn't got a snowball's chance in hell of making a go of Cyrus's place. But I never saw a woman so determined, so stubborn..."

"You admire her," Katoya said.

"I don't... Yes, I do," he admitted with a disbelieving shake of his head. Nathan kept his face averted from the Indian woman as he continued, "But I can't imagine why. She's setting herself up for a fall. I just hate to see her have to take it."

"We always have choices. Is there truly nothing that can be done?"

"Are you suggesting I offer to help her out?" Nathan demanded incredulously. "Because I won't. I'm not going to volunteer a shoulder to cry on, let alone one to carry a yoke. I've learned my lessons well," he said bitterly. "I'm not going to let that woman get under my skin."

"Perhaps it is too late. Perhaps you already care for her. Perhaps you will have no choice in the matter."

Nathan's jaw flexed as he ground his teeth. The Indian woman was more perceptive than was comfortable. How could he explain to her the feeling of possessiveness, of protectiveness that had arisen the moment he'd seen Harry-et Alistair. He didn't understand it himself. Hell, yes, he already cared about Harry-et Alistair. And that worried the dickens out of him. What if he succumbed to her allure? What if he

ended up getting involved with her, deeply, emotionally involved with her, and it turned out she needed
more than he could give? He knew what it meant to
have someone solely dependent upon him, to have
someone rely upon him for everything, and to know
that no matter how much he did it wouldn't be
enough. Nathan couldn't stand the pain of that kind
of relationship again.

"You must face the truth," Katoya said. "What will
be must be."

The old woman's philosophy was simple but irre-
futable. "All right," Nathan said. "I'll go see her
again tomorrow morning. But that doesn't mean I'm
going to get involved in her life."

Nathan repeated that litany until he fell asleep,
where he dreamed of a woman with freckles and
braids and bibbed overalls who kissed with a passion
that had made his pulse race and his body throb. He
woke up hard and hungry. He didn't shave, didn't eat,
simply pulled on jeans, boots, shirt, hat and coat and
slammed out the door.

When he arrived at the Alistair place, it was deathly
quiet. There was no smoke coming from the stone
chimney, no sounds from the barn, or from the tiny,
dilapidated cabin.

Something's wrong!

Nathan thrust the pickup truck door open and hit
the ground running for the cabin. His heart was in his
throat, his breath hard to catch because his chest was
constricted.

Let her be all right, he prayed. *I promise I'll help if only she's all right!*

The kitchen door not only wasn't locked, it wasn't even closed. Nathan shoved it open and roared at the top of his voice, "Harry-et! Are you in here? Harry-et!"

That was when he saw her. She was sitting on the floor, in the corner, with a lamb clutched to her chest, her eyes wide with terror at the sight of him. He was so relieved, and so angry that she had frightened him for nothing, that he raced over, grabbed her by the shoulders and hauled her to her feet.

"What the hell do you think you're doing, leaving the back door standing wide open? You'll catch your death of cold," he yelled, giving her shoulders a shake to make his point. "Of all the stupid, idiotic, green-horn—"

And then it dawned on him what he was doing, and he let her go as abruptly as he'd grabbed her. She backed up to the wall and stood there, staring at him.

Harry Alistair had a death grip on the lamb in her arms. There were dark circles under her eyes, which were wide and liquid with tears that hadn't yet spilled. Her whole body was trembling with fatigue and the aftereffects of the shaking Nathan had given her. Her mouth was working but the words weren't coming out in much more than a whisper.

Nathan leaned closer to hear what she was trying to say.

"Get out," she rasped. And then, stronger, "Get out of my house."

Nathan felt his heart miss a thump. "I'm sorry. Look, I only came over—"

Her chin came up. "I don't care why you came. I want you to leave. And don't come back."

Nathan's lips pressed flat. *What will be must be.* It was just as well things had turned out this way. It would have been a mistake to try to help her, anyway. But there was a part of him that died inside at the thought of not seeing her again. He wanted her. More than he had ever wanted another woman in his life. But she was all wrong for him. She needed the kind of caretaking he had sworn he was through with forever.

It took every bit of grit he had to turn on his booted heel and walk out of the room. And out of her life.

Three

———

What is accepted dress-for-success garb for country women?
Answer: Coveralls, scabby work shoes, holey hat and shredded gloves.

I am not a failure. I can do anything I set my mind to do. I will succeed.

Over the next two months there were many times when Harry wanted to give up. Often, it was only the repetition of those three sentences that kept her going. For, no matter how hard she tried, things always went awry. She had been forced to learn some hard lessons, and learn them fast.

About a week after the majority of the lambs had been born most of them got sick. Harry called in the

vet, who diagnosed lamb scours and prescribed anti-
biotics. Despite her efforts a dozen more lambs died.
She stacked them under the tarp beside the barn.

Early on the lambs had to have their tails docked,
and the ram lambs, except those valuable enough to be
sires, had to be castrated. Several of the older brochures described cutting off the lamb tails with a knife
and searing the stump with a hot iron. Castration was
described even more graphically. Faced with such
onerous chores, Harry had known she would never
make it as a sheepman.

At her lowest moment a brochure, describing a
more modern technique for docking and castration,
mysteriously arrived in her mailbox. An "elastrator"
and rubber bands were placed on the appropriate ex-
tremities, which wasted away and dropped off on their
own within two to three weeks. She found the process
unpleasant, time-consuming work. But with the information provided in the timely brochure, she had
succeeded when she might have given up.

Unfortunately Harry also lost several ewes during
delivery and found herself with more orphan lambs,
which she had learned were called bums, that had to
be fed with milk replacer. Bottle-feeding lambs turned
out to be surprisingly expensive. She had to dip into
the meager financial reserves Cyrus had left in the
bank. She would have run out of money except that
Harley's Feed Store had been having a sale on milk
replacer. That had seemed a little odd to Harry, but a
blushing Slim had assured her that he'd ordered too

much replacer, and if he didn't sell it cheap, it was just going to sit on the shelf for another year. Cyrus's money had gone farther than she had dared to hope.

It was a month of exhausting days and nights before Harry could wean the lambs to a solid feed of pellet rations. But she had made it. She still had money in the bank, and the lambs had all gotten fed. In fact, Harry was still bottle-feeding some that had been born late in the season. She had forgotten what it was like to get more than four hours of sleep in a row. When there was work to be done, she would repeat those three pithy sentences. They kept her awake and functioning despite what felt very much like battle fatigue. But then, wasn't she engaged in the greatest battle of her life?

By now even a novice like Harry had figured out that in its best days, Cyrus's sheep ranch had been a marginal proposition. With all the neglect over the years, it took every bit of time and attention she had to give simply to keep her head above water. But she was still afloat. And paddling for all she was worth. She hadn't failed. Yet. With a lot of hard work, and more than a little luck, she just might surprise everyone and make a go of Cyrus's ranch.

In the brief moments when Harry wasn't taking care of livestock—she had six laying hens, a rooster, a sow with eight piglets and a milk cow, as well as the sheep to attend—she had thought over her last meeting with Nathan Hazard.

Perhaps if she hadn't been quite so tired the morning he had come to see her, or if he hadn't woken her quite so abruptly, or been quite so upset, she might have been able to listen to what he had to say. If he had offered help, she might have accepted. She would never know for sure. Harry hadn't seen hide nor hair of him since.

Nor had anyone else come to visit. She had made a number of phone calls to John Wilkinson at the bank for advice, and had managed to get a few more tidbits of information from Slim every time she made a trip to Harley's Feed Store. But, quite frankly, Harry was beginning to feel the effects of the extreme isolation in which she had been living for the past two months.

Which was probably why she hadn't argued more when her mother, father and brother had said they were coming out to Montana to visit her. Unfortunately, with the time it had taken her to finish her chores this morning, she only had about fifteen minutes left to put herself together before she had to meet them at The Grand, the bed-and-breakfast in Big Timber where they were staying.

The varnished wooden booths that lined one wall of the luncheon dining room at The Grand had backs high enough to conceal the occupants and give them privacy. Thus, it wasn't until Nathan heard her exuberant greeting that he realized who was soon to occupy the next booth.

"Mom, Dad, Charlie, it's so good to see you!" Harry said.

"I'm sorry I can't say the same, darling," an uppity-sounding woman replied in a dismayed voice. "You look simply awful. What have you done to yourself? And what on earth is that you have on your head?"

Nathan smiled at the thought of Harry-et in her Harley's Feed Store cap.

A young man joined in with, "For Pete's sake, Harriet! Are you really wearing bibbed overalls?"

Nathan grinned. Very likely she was.

Before Harry had a chance to respond, an older man's bass voice contributed, "I knew I should have put my foot down. I didn't think you could manage on your own in this godforsaken place. And from the look of you, I wasn't wrong. When are you coming home?"

Nathan listened for Harriet's answer to that last question with bated breath.

There was a long pause before she answered, "I am home. And I have no intention of going back to Williamsburg, if that's what you're asking, Dad."

Nathan took advantage of the stunned silence that followed her pronouncement to take a quick swallow of coffee. He knew he ought not to eavesdrop on the Alistairs, but it wasn't as though he had come here with that thought in mind. He'd been minding his own business when *they'd* interrupted *him*. He signaled Dora Mae for a refill of his coffee and settled back to relax for a few minutes after lunch as was his custom.

He didn't listen, exactly, but he couldn't help but hear what was being said.

"I've been to see John Wilkinson at the bank," her father began. "And he—"

"Dad! You had no right—"

"I have every right," he interrupted. "I'm your father. I—"

"In case you haven't noticed, I'm not a child anymore," Harry interrupted right back. "I can take of myself."

"Darling," her mother said soothingly, "take a good, close look at yourself. There are dark circles under your eyes, your fingernails are chipped and broken and those awful clothes you're wearing are filthy. All I can conclude is that you're not taking good care of yourself. Your father and I only want the best for you. It hurts us to think of you suffering like this for nothing when in the end you'll only fail."

"I'm *not* suffering!" Harry protested. "And I will *not* fail. In fact, I'm doing just fine." That might have been an overstatement, but it was in a good cause.

"Fine?" her father questioned. "You can't possibly know enough about sheep ranching to succeed on your own. Why, even ranchers who know what they're doing sometimes fail."

"Dad..."

Nathan heard the fatigue and frustration in Harryet's voice. Her father shouldn't be allowed to browbeat her like that. Nathan ignored the Western code that admonished him not to interfere, in favor of the one that said a woman must always be protected. A moment later he was standing beside the next booth.

Harry was explaining, "I know what I'm doing, Dad. I've been reading all the brochures I can find about sheep ranching—"

"And she's had help from her neighbors whenever she ran into trouble," Nathan finished. A charming smile lit his face as he tipped his hat to Mrs. Alistair and said, "Howdy, ma'am. I'm Nathan Hazard, a neighbor of your daughter's."

Nathan bypassed Harry's stunned expression and turned an assessing gaze to her father and brother. "I couldn't help overhearing you, sir," he said to Harry's father. "And I just want to say that we've all been keeping an eye on Harry-et to make sure—"

"You've been what?"

Nathan turned to Harry, who had risen from her seat and was staring at him with her eyes wide and her mouth hanging open in horror.

"I was just saying that we've been keeping a neighborly eye on you." Before Harry could respond he had turned back to her father and continued, "You see, sir, we have a great deal of respect for women out here, and there isn't a soul in the valley who would stand by if he thought Harry-et was in any real trouble.

"Of course, you're right that she probably won't be able to make a go of Cyrus Alistair's place. But then it's doubtful whether anyone could. That's why I've offered to buy the place from her. And I have every hope that once she's gotten over the silly notion that—"

"Don't say another word!" Harry was so hot she could have melted icicles in January. She hung on to her temper long enough to say, "Mom, Dad, Charles, I hope you'll excuse us. I have a few words to say to Mr. Hazard. Alone."

Harry turned and stalked out to the front lobby of The Grand without waiting to see whether Nathan followed her. After tipping his hat once more to Mrs. Alistair, he did.

Just as Harry turned and opened her mouth to speak, Nathan took her by the elbow and started upstairs with her.

"Where do you think you're going?" Harry snapped, tugging frantically against his hold.

"Upstairs."

"There are *bedrooms* upstairs!"

"Yep. Sarah keeps all the doors open to show off her fancy antiques. We can use one of the rooms for a little privacy." He pulled her into the first open bedroom and shut the door behind them. "Now what's on your mind?"

"What's on my—?" Harry was so furious that she was gasping for air. "How dare you drag me up here—"

"We can go back downstairs and argue. That way everyone in the valley will know your business," he said, reaching for the doorknob.

"Wait!" Harry made the mistake of touching his hand and felt an arc of heat run up her arm. She jerked her hand away and took two steps back from him, only to come up against the edge of the ornate brass bed. She stepped forward again, only to find herself toe-to-toe with Nathan.

"Hold on a minute," she said, trying desperately to regain the upper hand. "How dare you insinuate to my family that I haven't been making it on my own! I most certainly have!"

Nathan shook his head.

"Don't try to deny it!" she retorted. "I haven't seen a soul except Slim Harley for the past two months. Just who, may I ask, has been helping me?"

"Me."

Harry was so stunned that she took a step back. When the backs of her legs hit the bed, she sat down. Her eyes never left Nathan's face, so she saw the flash of guilt in his blue eyes and the tinge of red growing on his cheeks. "You helped me? How?"

Nathan lifted his hat and shoved his fingers through his hair in agitation, then pulled his hat down over his brow again. "Little ways."

"How?"

He cleared his throat and admitted, "Dropped off a brochure once. Broke the ice on your ponds."

That explained some things she had wondered about. She had needed the knowledge the farm brochure had provided, but it wasn't as though he'd come over and helped with the docking and castration of the lambs. And while she had appreciated having the ice broken on her ponds, she could have done that herself. His interference didn't amount to as much as she had feared.

"And I talked Slim into putting his milk replacer on sale," he finished.

That was another matter entirely. Without the sale on milk replacer she'd have run out of money for sure. "You're responsible for that?"

"Wasn't a big deal. He really did order too much."

"Did anybody else get their milk replacer on sale?" she asked in a strained voice.

"No."

Harry's chest hurt. She couldn't breathe. "Why did you bother if you were so certain I'd fail in the end?"

"Thought you'd come to your senses sooner than this," he said gruffly. "Figured there was no sense letting all those lambs starve."

Harry turned to stare out a window draped with antique lace curtains. Her hand gripped the brass bedstead so hard that her knuckles were white. "Did it ever occur to you that I'd rather not have your help? Did it ever occur to you that whether I was going to fail or succeed I would rather do it all by myself?"

Nathan didn't know how to answer her. He willed her to look up at him, but he could tell how she felt even without seeing her face. Her pulse pounded in her throat and her jaw worked as she ground her teeth.

To tell the honest truth, he didn't know why he'd interfered in her life. If he had just left well enough alone, she would probably have quit and gone home a long time ago. Maybe that had something to do with it. Maybe he didn't want her to go away. He still felt the same attraction every time he got anywhere near her. And it was impossible to control his protective instincts whenever she was around. Just look what had happened today.

He reached out to touch her on the shoulder, and she jumped like a scalded cat. Only, when she came up off the bed she ran right flat into him. Instinctively his arms surrounded her.

The only sound in the room was the two of them breathing. Panting, actually, as though they had just run a footrace. Nathan didn't dare move, for fear she would bolt. It felt good holding her. He wanted more. Slowly, ever so slowly, he raised a hand and brushed his knuckles across her cheek. It was so smooth!

She looked up at him then, and he saw her pupils were wide, her eyes dark. Her mouth was slightly open, her lips full. Her eyelids closed as he lowered his mouth to touch hers. He felt the tremor run through her as their lips made contact. Soft. So incredibly soft, and moist.

When he ran his tongue along the edge of her mouth, she groaned. And her mouth opened wider to let him in.

He took his time kissing her, letting his lips learn the touch and taste of her. He felt the tension in her body, felt her resistance even as she succumbed to the desire that flared between them.

Nathan felt the same war within himself that he knew she was fighting. Lord, how he wanted her! And knew he shouldn't! But there was something about her, something about the touch and taste of her, that drew him despite his resolve not to become involved.

When he broke the kiss at last, she leaned her forehead against his chest. All the starch seemed to come out of her. "Why did you do that?" she asked in a whisper.

"I can't explain it myself. I don't want . . . I don't think we're very well suited to each other." He felt her tense again in his arms. "I don't mean to hurt your feelings. I'm only telling you the truth as I see it."

Harry dropped her hands, which she discovered were clutching either side of Nathan's waist, and stepped away from him. She raised her eyes to meet his steady gaze. "I can't disagree with you. I don't think we're well suited, either. I can't explain . . ." A rueful smile tilted her mouth up on one side. "You're quite good at kissing. You must have had a lot of practice."

Harry didn't realize she was fishing for information until the words were out of her mouth. She wanted to know if she was only one of many.

"I . . . uh . . . don't have much time for this sort of thing," he admitted. "Kissing women. A relationship with a woman, I mean."

"Oh?"

"Haven't had time for years," he blurted.

Harry was fascinated by the red patches that began at Nathan's throat and worked their way up. But his admission, however much it embarrassed him, gave Harry a reason for their tremendous attraction to each other. "I think I know why this...thing...is so strong between us," Harry said, as though speaking about it could diffuse its power.

This time Nathan said, "Oh?"

"Yes, you see, I haven't had much time for a relationship with a man. That has to be it, don't you agree? We have these normal, primitive urges, and we just naturally—"

"Naturally kiss each other every time we meet?" Nathan said with disbelief.

"Have you got a better explanation?" Harry demanded. Her fists found her hips in a stance that Nathan recognized all too well.

He shrugged. "I can't explain it at all. All I can say is I don't plan to let this happen again."

"Well, that's good to hear," Harry said. "Now that we have that settled, I'm going back downstairs to inform my family that I am managing fine *on my own*. And you will not contradict me. Is that clear?"

"Perfectly."

"Let's go, Mr. Hazard." She opened the door, waited for him to leave, then followed him toward the stairs.

"Wait!" He turned and she collided with his chest. His arms folded around her. The desire flared between them faster than they could stop it. Nathan swore under his breath as he steadied Harry and stepped back away from her.

"I only wanted to say," he said harshly, "that if you plan to stay in the valley, you'd better get your fallow fields planted with some kind of winter forage."

Harry wrapped her arms around herself as though that would protect her from the feeling roiling inside. "I'll do that. Is that all?"

He opened his mouth to say something about the stack of dead lambs beside her barn and shut it again. She had already asked Slim Harley what to do about them. He didn't understand why she hadn't buried them yet, but the closed expression on her face didn't encourage any more advice, let alone the offer of help he'd been about to make. "That's all," he said.

Nathan made his way back downstairs to the bar without once looking at Harry again. As he passed her family, he merely tipped his hat, grim-faced, and resumed his seat in the high-backed booth next to theirs.

Harry made quick work of reassuring her family that she was fine, and that she wouldn't be leaving Montana. There was no sound from the next booth. But Harry knew Nathan was there. And that he was listening.

"We'd like to see where you're living," her brother said. "What's it like?"

"Rustic," Harry said, her smile reappearing for the first time since she had entered The Grand.

"It sounds charming," her mother said.

"That it is," Harry said, her sense of humor making her smile broaden. "I'm afraid I can't invite you out to visit. It's a little small. And it doesn't have much in the way of amenities."

She heard Nathan snort in the next booth.

"Well, I feel better knowing your neighbors are keeping an eye on you," her father said. "That Hazard fellow seems a nice enough man."

Harry didn't think that deserved further comment, so she remained silent.

"Are you sure you can handle the financial end of things?" her father asked. "Mr. Wilkinson said you've got a big bill due next month for—"

"I can handle things, Dad," Harry said. "Don't worry."

She watched her father gnaw on his lower lip, then pull at the bushy white mustache that covered his upper lip. "All right, Harriet. If you insist on playing this game out to the bitter end, I suppose we have no choice except to go along—for now. But I think I should warn you, that if you aren't showing some kind of profit by the fall, I'll have to insist that you forget this foolishness and come home before winter sets in."

Harry was mortified to think that Nathan was hearing her father's ultimatum. She was tempted to let his words go without contesting them. That was the sort of passive resistance she had resorted to in the past. But the Harry who had come to Montana had turned over a new leaf. She felt compelled to say, "You're welcome to come and visit in the fall, Dad. I expect you'll be pleasantly surprised at how well I'm doing by then. But don't expect me to leave if I'm not."

Harry allowed her mother to admonish her to take better care of herself before she finally said, "I have to be getting back to the ranch. I've got stock that needs tending."

She rose and hugged her mother, father and brother, wishing things could be different, that she hadn't lived her life by pretending to fail. She would prove she could make it on her own if it was the last thing she did. Harry wished her family a pleasant drive from Big Timber to the airport in Billings, and a safe flight home. "I'll be in touch," she promised.

They would never know the effort it took to summon the confident smile with which she left them. "Things should be less hectic for me later in the summer," she said. "I'll look forward to seeing you then."

She could tell from their anxious faces that they didn't want to leave her in Montana alone. She reassured them the best she could with, "I'm all right, really. A little tired from all the hard work. But I love what I'm doing. It's challenging. And rewarding."

Harry smiled and waved as she left the restaurant. She was out the door before she realized Nathan Hazard had been standing behind her left shoulder the whole time she'd been waving goodbye.

"I'll follow you home," he said.

"Why on earth would you want to do that?"

Nathan looked up at a sky that was dark with storm clouds. "Looks like rain. All those potholes in your road, you could get stuck."

"If I do, Mr. Hazard, I'll dig myself out." Harry indignantly stalked away, but had to yank three or four times on the door to Cyrus's battered pickup before she finally got inside. She spent the entire trip home glaring at Nathan Hazard's pickup in her rearview mirror. He followed her all the way up to the tiny cabin door.

Harry hopped out of the pickup and marched back to Nathan's truck. He had the window down and his elbow stuck out.

"Rain, huh?" Harry said, looking up as the sun peered through the clouds, creating a glare on his windshield.

"Could have."

"Sheep dip," Harry said succinctly. "I've had it with helpful neighbors. From now on I want you to stay off my property. Stay away from me, and don't do me any more favors!"

"All right, Harry-et," he said with a long-suffering sigh. "We'll do it your way. For a while."

"For good!" Harry snapped back.

It was doubtful Nathan heard her, because he had already turned his pickup around and was headed back down the jouncy dirt road.

Harry kicked at a stone and sent it flying across the barren yard. Yes, the work was hard, and yes, she was tired. But she had loved every minute of the challenge she had set for herself. Before her talk with Nathan Hazard today she had indulged fully in the satisfaction of knowing she had done it all by herself. Darn him! Darn his interference! Darn the man for being such a darn good kisser!

If Nathan Hazard knew what was good for him, he wouldn't show his face around here anytime soon.

Four

———

What do you do when people drop by to visit and they haven't been invited?
Answer: Serve them coffee.

Harry was standing in the pigpen, slopping the hogs and thinking about Nathan, when she spied a pickup bumping down the dirt road that led to her place. At first she feared it was her nemesis and began tensing for another battle with Nathan. But the battered truck wasn't rusted in the right places to be Nathan's. After two months of being left so completely alone, Harry was surprised to have visitors. She couldn't help wondering who had come to see her, and why.

The man who stepped out of the driver's side of the beat-up vehicle was a stranger. Harry stood staring as a beautiful woman dressed in form-fitting jeans and a fleece-lined denim jacket shoved open the passenger door of the truck. The couple exchanged a glance that led Harry to believe they must be married, probably some of her neighbors, finally come to call.

The slight blond woman approached her and said, "Hello, I'm Abigail Dayton. Fish and Wildlife Service."

Harry was dumbfounded. *The woman was a government official!* What on earth was someone from the Fish and Wildlife Service doing here? Her heart caught in her throat, keeping her from responding. Her mind searched furiously for the reason for such a visit. Had she done something wrong? Broken some law? Forgotten to fill out some form? Had she let too many lambs die? Was there a penalty for that?

Harry recognized the instinct to flee and fought it. She had come west to start over, to confront her problems and deal with them. She would have to face this woman and find out what she wanted. Only first she had to get out of the pigpen, which wasn't as easy as it sounded.

Harry finally resorted to climbing over the top of the pen instead of going through the gate, which was wired shut. She heard a rip when her overalls caught on a stray barb, but ignored it as she extended her hand to the Fish and Wildlife agent. When the woman didn't take her hand immediately, Harry realized she was still wearing her work gloves, tore them off and tried again. "I'm Harriet Alistair. People mostly call me Harry."

"It's nice to meet you, Harry," Abigail said. She shook Harry's hand once, then let it go.

Harry turned and looked steadily at the tall, dark-haired, gray-eyed man standing beside Abigail Dayton, until he finally held out a calloused hand and said, "I'm Luke Granger, your neighbor to the south. Sorry I haven't been over to see you sooner."

Harry was so glad Luke Granger was just a neighbor and not another government official that she smiled, exposing the tiny space between her teeth, and said, "I've been pretty busy myself. It's good to meet you."

So, one agent, one neighbor. Not related. But still no explanation as to why they had come.

Harry felt a growing discomfort as she watched Luke and Abigail survey her property. It wasn't that they openly displayed disgust or disbelief at what they saw; in fact, they were both careful to keep their expressions neutral. But a tightening of Luke's jaw, and a clenching of Abigail's hand, made their feelings plain. Harry wasn't exactly ashamed of her place. After all, she was hardly responsible for the sad state of repairs. But her stomach turned over when Abigail narrowed her green-eyed gaze on the stack of dead lambs beside the barn that were only partially covered by a black plastic tarp. Harry waited for the official condemnation that was sure to come.

"Have you seen any wolves around here?" Abigail asked.

"Wolves?" That wasn't at all what Harry had been expecting the Fish and Wildlife agent to say. The thought of wolves somewhere on her property was terrifying. "Wolves?" she repeated.

"A renegade timber wolf killed two of Luke's sheep," Abigail continued. "I wondered if you've suffered any wolf depredation on your spread."

"Not that I know of," Harry said. "I didn't even know there were any wolves around here."

"There aren't many," Abigail reassured her. "And there's going to be one less as soon as I can find and capture the renegade that killed Luke's sheep."

Harry watched a strange tension flare between her two visitors at Abigail's pronouncement. Before Harry had time to analyze it further, Abigail asked, "Have you seen any wolf sign at all?"

Harry grimaced and shook her head. "I wouldn't know it if I saw it. But you're welcome to take a look around."

"I think I will if you really don't mind."

Abigail carefully looked the grounds over, with Luke by her side. Harry did her best to keep them headed away from the tiny log cabin. She had already tasted their disapproval once and was reluctant to have them observe the primitive conditions under which she lived. However, before Harry knew it, they were all three standing at her kitchen door; there wasn't much she could do except invite them inside.

Harry felt a flush of embarrassment stain her cheeks when both Luke and Abigail stopped dead just inside the door. The scene that greeted them in the kitchen was pretty much the same one that had greeted Nathan the first time he'd come to visit. Only now there were six lambs sleeping on a blanket wadded in the corner instead of just one. The shambles in Harry's kitchen gave painful evidence of how hard she was struggling to cope with the responsibilities she had assumed on Cyrus Alistair's death. Harry didn't know what to say. What could she say?

Abigail finally broke the looming silence. "I'd love some coffee. Wouldn't you, Luke?"

Grateful for the simple suggestion, Harry urged her company to seat themselves at the kitchen table. While she made coffee, Harry lectured herself about how it didn't really matter what these people thought. The important thing was that she had survived the past two months.

Harry poured three cups of coffee and brought them to the table, then seated herself across from Abigail, who was saying something about how wolves weren't really as bad as people thought, and how their reputation had been exaggerated by all those fairy tales featuring a Big Bad Wolf.

Harry wasn't convinced. She took a sip of the hot, bitter coffee and said, "I've been meaning to learn how to use a rifle in case I had trouble with predators, but—"

Abigail leaped up out of her chair in alarm. "You can't *shoot* a timber wolf! They're an endangered species. They're protected!"

"I'm sorry!" Harry said. "I didn't know." She shook her head in disgust. "There's just so much I don't know!"

Abigail sat back down a little sheepishly. "I'm afraid I tend to get on my high horse whenever the discussion turns to wolves."

Harry ran her fingers aimlessly across the pamphlets and brochures that littered the table, shouting her ignorance of sheep ranching to anyone who cared to notice.

"You really shouldn't leave those dead lambs lying around, though," Abigail said. "They're liable to attract predators."

Harry chewed on her lower lip. "I know I'm supposed to bury them, but I just can't face the thought of doing it."

"I've got some time right now," Luke said. "Why don't you let me help?"

Harry leaned forward to protest. "But I can't pay—"

"Neighbors don't have to pay each other for lending a helping hand," he said brusquely. A moment later he was out the door.

"You know, I bet there's a really nice man behind that stony face he wears," Harry said as she stared after him.

"I wouldn't know," Abigail said. "I only met him this morning."

"Oh, I thought…" Harry didn't finish her thought, discouraged by the shuttered look on Abigail's face. There was something going on between Luke and Abigail, all right. But if they'd just met, the sparks must have been pretty instantaneous. Just like the desire that had flared between her and Nathan. Harry felt an immediate affinity to the other woman. After all, they had both been attracted to rough-hewn Montana sheepmen.

Abigail rose and took her coffee cup to the sink, and without Harry quite being aware how it happened, Abigail was soon washing the mound of dirty dishes, while Harry dried then and put them away. While they worked, they talked, and Harry found herself confiding to Abigail, "Sometimes I wake up in the morning and I wonder how long it'll take me to get this place into shape, or if I ever will."

"Why would you want to?" Abigail blurted. "I mean… To be perfectly frank this place needs a lot of work."

Harry's sense of humor got the better of her, and she grinned. "That's an understatement if I ever heard one. This place is a *wreck.*"

"So tell me why you're staying," Abigail urged.

"It's a long story."

"I'd like to hear it."

Harry took a deep breath and let it out. "All right."

It was a tremendous relief to Harry to be able to tell someone—someone who had no reason to be judgmental—how she had lived her life. Abigail's interested green eyes and sympathetic oohs and ahs helped Harry relate the various fiascos that littered her past. It wasn't until she started talking about Nathan Hazard that words became really difficult to find.

"At first I was so grateful he was there," Harry said as she explained how Nathan had helped in the birthing of the dead lamb and its twin. "I think that was why I was so angry when it turned out he had only come because he wanted to buy this place from me. I'm determined to manage on my own, but the man keeps popping up when I least expect him. And somehow, every time we've crossed paths, we end up—"

"End up what?"

"Kissing," Harry admitted. "I know that sounds absurd—"

"Not so absurd as you think," Abigail muttered. "Must be more to these Montana sheepmen then meets the eye," she said with a rueful smile.

"Nathan Hazard is driving me crazy," Harry said. What she didn't add, couldn't find words to explain, was how every time she inevitably ended up in his arms, the fire that rose between them seemed unquenchable. "I wish he would just leave me alone."

That wasn't precisely true. What she wanted was a different kind of attention from Nathan Hazard than she was getting. Something more personal and less professional. But that was too confusing, and much too complicated, to contemplate.

Harry looked around her and was amazed to discover that while she had been talking Abigail had continued doing chores around the kitchen. The dishes were washed, the floor was swept, the counters were clear and the brochures on the table had been separated into neat stacks. Several lambs had woken, and Abigail had matter-of-factly joined Harry on the floor to help her bottle-feed the noisy bums.

"Have you thought about getting a hired hand to help with the heavy work?" Abigail asked.

"Can't afford one," Harry admitted. "Although Mr. Wilkinson at the bank said there's a shepherd who'll keep an eye on my flock once I get it moved onto my federal lease in the mountains for the summer. Anyway, I'm determined to make it on my own."

"That's a laudable goal," Abigail said, "but is it realistic?"

"I thought so," Harry mused. "Since I didn't know a thing about sheep ranching when I arrived in Montana, I've made my share of mistakes. But I'm learning fast."

"You don't have to answer if you don't want to," Abigail said, "but why on earth don't you just sell this place—"

"To Nathan Hazard? Don't get me started again. I'll never sell to that man. Nathan Hazard is the meanest, ugliest son of a—"

Harry never got a chance to finish her sentence because Luke arrived at the door and announced, "I've buried those lambs. Anything else you'd like me to do while I'm here?"

"No thanks," Harry said, scrambling to her feet. "We're about finished here." She put the empty nippled Coke bottle on the kitchen counter and said, "I really appreciate your help, Luke."

"You're welcome, anytime."

It took a moment for Harry to realize that although Luke was speaking to her, his attention was totally absorbed by the woman still sitting on the floor feeding the last ounce of milk replacer to a hungry lamb. From the look on Luke's face it appeared he would gladly take the lamb's place. Harry had wondered why Luke had come visiting with the Fish and Wildlife agent. Now she had her answer.

Harry was envious of what she saw in Luke Granger's eyes. No man had ever looked at her with such raw hunger, such need.

Unless you counted Nathan Hazard.

Harry watched as Abigail raised her eyes to Luke, a beatific smile on her face, watched as the smile faded, watched as Abigail's eyes assumed the wary look of an animal at bay.

Luke's gray eyes took on a feral gleam; his muscles tensed and coiled in readiness.

The hunter. And the hunted. Harry recognized the relationship because she had felt it herself. With Nathan Hazard.

An instant later Luke reached out a hand and pulled Abigail to her feet. Harry was uncomfortably aware of the frisson of sexual attraction that arced between them as they touched. She observed their cautious movements as Abigail inched past Luke in the tiny kitchen and joined Harry at the sink.

"I suppose Luke and I should get going," Abigail said. "We've got a few more ranchers to ask about wolf sightings before the day's done. I've enjoyed getting to know you, Harry. I wish you luck with your ranch."

"Thanks," Harry said with a smile as she escorted Abigail and Luke back outside. "I need all the luck I can get." She turned to Luke and said, "I hope you'll come back and visit again soon, neighbor."

"Count on it," he replied, tipping his Stetson.

"And I hope you capture that renegade wolf," Harry said to Abigail.

Harry watched as Abigail gave Luke a determined, almost defiant, look and said, "Count on it."

Abigail had trouble getting the passenger door of the pickup open, and Harry was just about to lend a hand when Luke stepped up and yanked it free. Abigail frowned at him and said, "I could have done that."

He shrugged. "Never said you couldn't." But he waited for her to get inside and closed the door snugly behind her before heading around to the driver's side of the truck.

"So long," Harry shouted after them as they drove away. "Careful on that road. It's a little bumpy!" A perfect farewell, Harry thought with an ironic twist of her mouth, seeing as how this had been a day for understatement.

Harry felt sorry to see them leave. She was probably being unnecessarily stubborn about trying to manage all by herself. Nathan Hazard was convinced she couldn't manage on her own. She could take advantage of Luke's offer of help and avoid making any more costly mistakes. But the whole purpose of coming to Montana, of putting herself in this isolated position, was to prove that she could do anything she set her mind to do *on her own*. She wasn't the person she had led her parents to believe she was. Harry had realized over the past two months that she wanted to prove that fact to herself even more than she wanted to prove it to them.

It would be too easy to stop resisting Nathan Hazard's interference in her business. Harry reminded herself that Nathan didn't really want her to succeed; he wanted Cyrus's land. And he wanted to take care of her, as one would care for someone incapable of taking care of herself. Letting Nathan Hazard into her life right now would be disastrous. Because Harry didn't want any more people taking care of her; she wanted to prove she could take care of herself.

Harry had another motive for wanting to keep Nathan at a distance. Whenever he was around she succumbed to the attraction she felt for him. At a time

when she was trying to take control of her life, the
feelings she had for Nathan Hazard were uncontrollable. She wanted to touch him, and have him touch
her, to kiss him and be kissed back with all the passion she felt whenever he held her in his arms, to share
with him and to have him share the feelings she was
hard put to name, but couldn't deny. Those powerful
emotions left her feeling threatened in a way she
couldn't explain. It was far better, Harry decided, to
keep the man at a distance.

The next time Nathan Hazard came calling, if there
was a next time, he wouldn't be welcome.

Harry woke the next day to the clang of metal on
metal. She bolted upright in bed, then sat unmoving
while she tried to place the sound. She couldn't, and
quickly pulled on a heavy flannel robe and stepped
into ice-cold slippers as she headed for the window to
look outside. Her jaw dropped at what she saw. Nathan Hazard stood bare-chested, wrench in hand,
working on the engine of Cyrus's farm tractor.

Her first thought was, he must be freezing to death!
Then she looked at the angle of the sun and realized it
had to be nearly midday and would be much warmer
outside than in the cabin, which held the cold. How
had she slept so long? The lambs usually woke her at
dawn to be fed. She hurried to the kitchen, and they
were all there—sleeping peacefully. A quick glance at
the kitchen counter revealed several empty nippled

Coke bottles. Nathan Hazard had been inside her house this morning! He had fed her lambs!

Harry felt outraged at Nathan's presumption. And then she had another, even more disturbing thought. Had he come into her bedroom? Had he seen her sleeping? She blushed at the thought of what she must have looked like. She had worn only a plain white torn T-shirt to sleep in Cyrus's sleigh bed. Harry was disgusted with herself when she realized that what upset her most was the thought that she couldn't have looked very attractive.

It took three shakes of a lamb's tail for Harry to dress in jeans, blue work shirt and boots. She stomped all the way from her kitchen door to the barn, where the tractor stood. Nathan had to hear her coming, but he never moved from his stance bent over concentrating on some part of the tractor's innards.

"Good morning!" she snarled.

Slowly, as though it were the most ordinary thing in the world for him to be working on her tractor, he straightened. "Good afternoon," he corrected.

Harry caught her breath at the sight of him. She didn't see the whole man, just perceptions of him. A bead of sweat slid slowly down the crease in his muscular chest to dampen the waist of his jeans. Only the waist wasn't at his waist. His jeans had slid down over his hips to reveal a navel and a line of downy blond hair that disappeared from sight under the denim; she didn't see any sign of underwear. The placket over the zipper was worn white with age. When she realized where she was staring, Harry jerked her head up to look at his face and noticed that a stubble of beard shadowed his jaws and chin. Hanks of white-blond hair were tousled over his forehead. And his shockingly bright blue eyes were focused on her as though she were a lamb chop and he were a starving man.

Harry's mouth went dry. She slicked her tongue over her lips and saw the resulting spark of heat in Nathan's gaze. His nostrils flared, and she felt her body tighten with anticipation. The hunter. Its prey. The scene was set.

Only Harry had no intention of becoming a sacrificial lamb to this particular wolf.

"Don't you know how to knock?" she demanded.

It might have seemed an odd question, but Nathan knew what she was asking. "I did knock. You didn't answer. I was worried, so I came inside."

"And fed my lambs!" Harry said indignantly.

"Yes. I fed them."

"Why didn't you come wake me up?"

Nathan had learned enough about Harry-et Alistair's pride to know he couldn't tell her the truth. She had looked tired. More than tired, exhausted. He had figured she could use the sleep. So he had fed her lambs. Was that so bad? Obviously Harry-et thought so.

But her need for sleep wasn't the only reason he hadn't woken her. When Nathan had entered Harry-et's bedroom, she was lying on her side, with one long, bare, elegantly slender leg curled up outside the blankets. The tiny bikini panties she'd been wearing had revealed a great expanse of hip, as well. Her long brown hair was spread across the pillow in abandon. One breast was pushed up by the arm she was lying on, and he had seen a dark nipple through the thin cotton T-shirt she was wearing. Not that he'd looked on purpose. Or very long. In fact, once he'd realized the full extent of her dishevelment, he had backed out of the room so fast he'd almost tripped over her work boots that lay where they'd fallen when she had taken them off the previous night.

He had wanted to wake her more than she would ever know. He had wanted to take her in his arms and feel her nipples against his bare chest. He had wanted to wrap those long, luscious legs around himself and... No, she was damn lucky he hadn't woken her. But he could never tell her that. Instead he said, "Anybody offered me another hour or two of sleep, I'd be grateful."

Harry sputtered, unable to think of an appropriate retort. She *was* grateful for the sleep. She just didn't like the way she'd gotten it. "What are you doing to this tractor?"

"Fixing it."

"I didn't know it was broken."

"Neither did I until I tried starting it up."

"Why would you want to start it up?"

Nathan leaned back over and began tinkering again, so he wouldn't have to look her in the eye when he said, "So I could plow your fallow fields."

"So you could..." Harry was flabbergasted. "I thought you were too busy doing your own work to lend me a hand."

Nathan stood and leaned a hip against the tractor while he wiped his hands on his chambray work shirt. "I had a visit yesterday from a good friend of mine, Luke Granger. He was with an agent of the Fish and Wildlife Service, Abigail—"

"They were here yesterday. So?"

"Luke pointed out to me that I haven't been a very good neighbor."

Harry felt her stomach churn. "What else did he have to say?"

"That was enough, don't you think?"

Harry met Nathan's solemn gaze and found it even more unsettling than the heat that had so recently been there.

Nathan never took his eyes off her when he added, "I think maybe I've been a little pigheaded about helping you out. On the other hand, Harry-et, I can't help thinking—"

The blaring honk of a truck horn interrupted Nathan. A battered pickup was wending its way up the rutted dirt road.

Harry recognized Luke Granger and Abigail Dayton. "I wonder what they're doing back here today?"

"I invited them."

Harry whirled to face Nathan. "You what?"

"I called Luke this morning to see if he could spare a little time to do some repairs around here." He took a look around the dilapidated buildings and added, "There's plenty here for both of us to do."

"You all got together and figured I needed help, so here you are riding to the rescue like cowboys in white hats," Harry said bitterly. "Darn. Oh, darn, darn, darn." Harry fisted her hands and placed them on her hips to keep from hauling off and hitting Nathan. She clamped her teeth tight to keep her chin from quivering. She wanted to scream and rant and rave. And she was more than a little afraid she was going to cry.

Nathan couldn't understand what all the fuss was about. In all the years he had been offering help to others, the usual response had been a quick and ready acceptance of his assistance. This woman was totally different. She seemed to resent his support. He found her reaction bewildering. And not a little frustrating. He should have been glad she didn't need his help. He should have been glad she didn't need any caretaking. But he found himself wanting to help, needing to help. Her rejection hurt in ways he wasn't willing to acknowledge. He turned and began working on the tractor again, keeping his hands busy to keep from grabbing Harry and kissing some sense into her.

"Hello, there," Luke said as he and Abigail approached the other couple.

"Hello," Harry muttered through clenched teeth. Her angry eyes remained on Nathan.

Nathan never looked up. "I ran into a little problem, Luke. The tractor needs some work before I can do anything about those fallow fields."

"Anything I can do?" Luke asked Nathan.

Harry whirled on him and said, "You can turn that truck around and drive right back out of here."

"We just want to help," Abigail said quietly.

"I don't need your charity," Harry cried in an anguished voice. "I don't need—"

Nathan suddenly dropped his wrench on the engine with a clatter and grabbed Harry by the arms, forcing her to face him. "That'll be enough of that!"

"Just who do you think you are?" Harry rasped. "I didn't ask you to come here. I didn't ask you to—"

"I'm doing what a good neighbor should do."

"Right! Where was all this neighborliness when I had lambs dying because I didn't know how to deliver them? Where was all this friendly help when I really needed it?"

"You need it right now," Nathan retorted, his grip tightening. "And I intend to give it to you."

"Over my dead body!" Harry shouted.

"Be reasonable," Nathan said in a voice that was losing its calm. "You need help."

"I don't need it from you," Harry replied stubbornly.

"Maybe you'd let us help," Abigail said, stepping forward to place a comforting hand on Harry's arm.

Harry's shoulders suddenly slumped, all the fight gone out of her. Maybe she should just take their help. Maybe her parents had been right all along. She bit her quivering lower lip and closed her eyes to hold back the threatening tears.

But some spark inside Harry refused to be quenched by the dose of reality she'd just suffered. She could give up, and give in, as she had in the past. Or she could fight. Her shoulders came up again, and when her eyes opened, they focused on Nathan Hazard, flashing with defiance. "I want you off my property, Nathan Hazard. Now. I..." Her voice caught in an angry sob, but her jaw stiffened. "I have things to do inside. I expect you can see yourself off my land."

Harry turned and marched toward the tiny log house without a single look back to see if he had obeyed her command.

Five

___

What do you say when asked, "How's it going?"
Answer: "Oh, could be worse. Could be better."

Nathan spent the rest of the afternoon working outside with Luke, while Abigail worked in and around the barn with a still-seething Harry. Luke and Abigail left just before sundown, knowing Harry's fallow fields were plowed and planted and that the pigpen gate, among other things, had been repaired. Nathan worked another quarter hour before admitting there wasn't enough light to continue. He pulled on the chambray shirt he'd been using for an oil rag and headed toward the only light on in Cyrus's log cabin.

He knocked at Harry's kitchen door, but didn't wait for an answer before he pushed the screen door open and stepped inside. Harry was standing at the sink rinsing out Coke bottles. She turned when she saw him, grabbed a towel from the counter and wiped her hands dry. She stood backed up against the sink, waiting, wary.

"I'm sorry." Nathan hadn't said those two words very often in his lifetime, and they stuck in his craw.

It didn't help when Harry retorted, "You should be!"

"Now look here, Harry-et—"

"No, *you* look here, Nathan," she interrupted. "I thought I'd made it plain to you that I didn't want your help. At least not the way you're offering it. I wouldn't mind so much if you wanted to teach me how to run this place. But you seem bound and determined to treat me like the worst sort of tenderfoot, which I am—a tenderfoot, I mean. But not the worst sort. Oh, this isn't making any sense!"

Harry was so upset that she gulped air, and she trembled as though she had the ague. Nathan took a step toward her, wanting to comfort her, but stopped when she stuck out a flat palm.

"Wait. I'm not finished talking. I don't know how to make it any plainer. I don't want the sort of help you're offering, Nathan."

Nathan opened his mouth to offer her the kind of help she was asking for and snapped it shut. Even if he taught her what she wanted to know, she would be hard-pressed to make a go of this place by herself. And if, by some miracle, she did succeed, he would only be stuck with another Alistair planted square in the middle of Hazard land.

"All right, Harry-et," he said, "I'll stop trying to help."

Her shoulders sagged, and he wasn't sure if she was relieved or disappointed. Neither reaction pleased him. So he said, "I think maybe what we ought to do is call a truce."

"A truce?"

"Yeah. You know, raise the white flag. Stop fighting. Call a halt to hostilities." He tried a smile of encouragement. It wasn't his best, but apparently it was good enough, because she smiled back.

"All right," she agreed. "Shall we shake on it?"

She stuck her hand out and, like a fool, he took it. And suffered the consequences. Touching her was like shooting off fireworks on the Fourth of July. He liked what he felt. Too much. So he dropped her hand and turned to leave. Before he even got to the door he had turned back—he didn't have the faintest idea why—and caught her looking bereft. The words were out of his mouth before he could stop them. "What would you say to a dinner to celebrate our truce?" She looked doubtfully around her kitchen, and he quickly added, "I meant dinner out."

"A date?"

"Not a date," he quickly reassured her. "Just a dinner between two neighbors who've agreed to make peace."

"All right."

It was the most reluctant acceptance he'd ever heard. Nathan figured he'd better get the plans finalized and get out of here before she changed her mind. "I'll pick you up at eight. Dress up fancy."

"Fancy?"

"Sure. Something soft and ladylike. You have a dress like that, don't you?" He hadn't realized how much he wanted to see her in a dress, so he could admire those long legs of hers again.

"Where is this dinner going to be?" she asked suspiciously.

"Have you ever been to the hot springs at Chico?"

"No. Where is that?"

"About an hour south. Best lamb chops in two counties." He saw her moue of distress and added, "Or you can have beef prime ribs if you'd rather."

She smiled, and he felt his heart beat faster at the shy pleasure revealed in the slight curl of her lips.

"All right. I'll be ready," she said.

Nathan left in a hurry before he did something really stupid, like take her in his arms and kiss that wide, soft mouth of hers and run his hands all over her body. He had it bad, all right. The worst. The woman was under his skin and there was no denying it.

Nathan drove home so fast that his head hit the top of the pickup twice on his way down Harry-et's road. He showered and shaved and daubed some manly-smelling, female-alluring scent on himself in record time. He donned a sandy-colored, tailored western suit that hugged him across the shoulders like a second

skin and added snakeskin boots and a buff felt cowboy hat.

Nathan wasn't conscious of how carefully he had
dressed until Katoya stopped him at the bottom of the
stairs and said, "You are going hunting."

"I'm not exactly dressed for bear."

"Not for bear. For dear. One dear," the old woman
clarified with a cackle of glee.

Nathan grimaced. "Is it that obvious?"

"Noticeable, yes. As a wolf among sheep."

He started back up the stairs again. "I'll change."

"It will do no good."

Nathan walked back down to her. "Why not?"

"Even if you change the outer trappings, she will
know what you feel."

"How?" he demanded.

"She will see it in your eyes. They shine with excitement. And with hunger."

Nathan looked down at his fisted hands so that his
lids would veil what the old woman had seen. "I want
her," he said. He looked up, and there was a plea in
his eyes he didn't know was there. "I know I'm asking for trouble. She's all wrong for me. But I can't
seem to stop myself."

"Maybe you shouldn't try," Katoya said softly.
"Maybe it is time you let go of the past."

"Wish I could," he said. "It isn't easy."

"We do the best we can," the Blackfoot woman
said. "Go. Enjoy yourself. What must be will be."

He grabbed the tiny woman and hugged her hard. "You're a wise old woman. I'll do my best to take your advice."

He let her go and hurried out the door, anxious to be on his way. He didn't see the sadness in her eyes as he left or the pain in her step as she headed for the window to watch him drive away in a classic black sports car that spent most of its time in his garage.

For the entire trip to Cyrus's ranch Nathan imagined how wonderful Harry-et would look dressed up. But the reality still exceeded his expectation.

"I can't believe it's you," he said in an awestruck voice when Harry opened the front door to the cabin. She stepped out, rather than inviting him in, and having seen the broken-down couch and chairs from the 1950s that served as living room furniture, Nathan understood why. But he wouldn't let Harry into his car until he'd taken a good look at her.

"Wait. Turn around."

"Do you like it?" she asked anxiously.

How could he describe how beautiful she looked to him? He didn't think he could find the words. "I love it," he managed.

The dress was a vibrant red and made of material that looked soft to the touch. The skirt was full, so it floated around her. The bodice was fitted, crisscrossing in a V over her breasts, so for the first time he could see just how lovely she was. The chiffonlike material fell off her shoulders, leaving them completely bare, but enticed with a hint of cleavage. She'd taken her hair out of the tomboyish braids, and a mass of rich brown curls draped her bare shoulders, begging to be taken up in his hands. She was wearing high heels that lengthened her already-long legs and brought her eyes almost even with his.

He could see how easy it would be to push the material down from her shoulders, leaving her breasts free to touch and taste. How easy it would be to slip his hands under the full skirt and capture her thighs, pulling her close. That thought pushed him over the edge. He felt himself responding to the wanton images that besieged him while she stood there looking lovely and desirable.

"Get in the car," he said in a voice harsh with the need he was struggling to control.

He hates the dress, Harry thought as she obeyed Nathan's curt order. She'd known the red dress was all wrong for her when she'd bought it two years ago. Too bright. Too sexy. Too sensual. Not at all like the Harriet Alistair of Williamsburg, Virginia. But tonight, when she'd looked into her closet, there it was. And it had seemed exactly right for the bold and daring woman who'd moved to Big Timber, Montana. The one who was attracted to Nathan Hazard.

Apparently Nathan didn't agree.

On the other hand, Harry thought Nathan looked wonderful. His western suit fit him to perfection. The tailoring showed off his broad shoulders and narrow hips, his flat stomach and long legs. Of course, she had never found any fault with the way Nathan looked. Indeed, she had wanted to touch the rippled chest and belly she'd seen this morning. Would Nathan's skin be soft? Or as hard as the muscles that corded his flesh? Harry had even fantasized what Nathan would look like without a stitch on. But she had never seen a naked man, and the only images she could conjure were the marble statues of Greek gods she had seen. And a leaf had always covered the pertinent parts.

Tonight there was a barely leashed power in the way Nathan moved that made Harry want to test the limits of his control. She wanted to touch. She wanted to taste. And she wanted to tempt Nathan to do the same.

Their personal relationship had nothing to do with the land, Harry told herself. It was separate and apart from that. She could desire Nathan without compromising her stand, because they were in the midst of a truce. So when she sat down in Nathan's sports car, she let her skirt slip halfway up her thighs before pulling it back down, and leaned toward Nathan so that her breast brushed against his arm.

He inhaled sharply.

Harry looked at him, stunned by the flood of desire in his eyes. And began to reevaluate Nathan's reaction to her red dress.

Nathan didn't leave her in doubt another moment. He leaned over slowly but surely until their mouths were nearly touching and said, "Don't do that again unless you mean it."

Harry shivered and made a little noise in her throat.

Nathan groaned as his lips covered hers and sipped the nectar there. Her mouth was soft and oh, so sweet, and his body tightened like a bowstring with need. His tongue found the edge of her lips and followed it until she opened her mouth and his tongue slipped inside. He mimed the stroke of their two bodies joined and heard her moan. He reached up a hand to cup her breast and felt the weight of it in his hand. His thumb stroked across the tip, and he realized it had already tightened into a tiny nub. His hand followed the shape of her, from her ribs to her waist and down her thigh to the hem of her skirt, where Harry caught his wrist and stopped him.

Abruptly Nathan lifted his mouth from hers. Damn if she didn't have him as hot and bothered as a high school kid! And she'd stopped him as if she were some teenage virgin who'd never done it before. On the other hand, though he felt like a kid, he wasn't one. The small car was damn close for comfort. He could wait. Before the night was through he'd know what it was like to hold her in his arms, and feel himself inside her. She wanted it. And so did he.

"All right, Ms. Alistair," he said through gritted teeth. "We'll do this your way."

Nathan started the car, made a spinning turn and, in deference to his delicate suspension, headed at a slow crawl back down the bumpy dirt road toward the main highway and Chico.

Harry was stunned. How had one kiss turned into so much so fast? She hadn't wanted to stop Nathan.

But things were moving too quickly. She didn't want the first time to be in the front seat of a car. They both deserved more than that.

Nathan was on the verge of suggesting they forget dinner and go back to his place. But from the nervous fidgeting Harry was doing, that probably wasn't a good idea. He figured he'd better say something quick before he said what was really on his mind. So he cleared his throat of the last remnants of passion and asked, "What was your life like before you came to Montana?"

"Overprotected."

Nathan glanced briefly at Harry-et to see if she was kidding. She wasn't. "I guess I saw a little of that when your parents were here. They sure don't think you can make a go of Cyrus's ranch, do they?"

"That isn't their fault," Harry said, coming to their defense. "I wasn't exactly what you'd call a roaring success when I lived in Williamsburg."

"What were you, exactly?"

Harry paused for a moment before she admitted, "I had several occupations, but I wasn't interested in any of them. I managed to do poorly at them, so I could get fired."

"Why did you take the jobs in the first place if you weren't interested in them?"

"Because I couldn't say no to my father."

Nathan snorted. "You haven't had any trouble saying no to me."

"I turned over a new leaf when I came to Montana," Harry said with an impish smile. "I made up my mind to do what I wanted to do, my way." Her expression became earnest. "That's why I was so upset by your interference. Don't you see? I wanted to prove to my family, and to myself, that I could succeed at something on my own."

"I'm sorry I butted in," Nathan said curtly.

Harry put a hand on Nathan's arm and felt him tense beneath her fingertips. "How could you know? Now that we've called this truce, things will be better, I'm sure. What about you? Did you always want to be a sheep rancher?"

"No. Actually, I had plans to be an architect once upon a time."

"What happened?"

Nathan glanced at Harry and was surprised by the concerned look on her face. He hardened himself against the growing emotional attachment he felt to her. "Things got in the way."

"What kind of things?"

"Parents."

"You weren't overprotected, too, were you?"

"Not hardly. I was the one who did the protecting in my household."

Harry was stunned by the bitterness in his voice. "I don't understand. Are you saying you took care of your parents? Were they hurt or something?"

"Yes, and yes."

But he didn't say any more. Harry wasn't sure whether to press him for details. His lips had flattened into a grim line, and the memories obviously weren't happy ones. But her curiosity got the better of her and she asked, "Will you tell me about it?"

At first she thought he wasn't going to speak. Then the words started coming, and the bitterness and anger and regret and sadness poured out along with them.

"My mother was an alcoholic," he said. "I didn't know her very well. But I took care of her the best I could. Dumped the bottles when I found them. Cleaned up when I could. Made meals for me and my dad. She didn't eat much. The alcohol finally killed her when I was sixteen.

"It was a relief," he said in a voice that grated with pain. "I was glad she was gone. She was an embarrassment. She was a lush. I hated her." Harry watched him swallow hard and add in a soft voice, "And I loved her so much I would have died in her place."

Harry felt a lump in her own throat and tears burning her eyes. What a heavy burden for a child!

"My father and I missed her when she was gone. Dad wanted me to stay on the ranch—Hazards had been sheep ranchers for a hundred years—but I wanted to be an architect. So I went away to college despite his wishes and learned to design buildings to celebrate the spirit of life.

"The month I graduated my father had an accident. A tractor turned over on him and crippled him.

I came home to take over for him. And to take care of him. That was fifteen years ago. He died two years ago an old man. He was fifty-eight.''

"Did you ever have the opportunity to design anything?"

"I designed and built the house I live in now. I haven't had time to do more than that."

She could hear the pride in his voice. And the disappointment. "I'm sorry."

"Don't pity me. I've had a good life. Better than most."

"But it wasn't the life you had planned for yourself. What about a wife? Didn't you ever want to marry and have children?"

"I was too busy until two years ago to think about anything but making ends meet," Nathan said. "Since then I've been looking. But I haven't found the right woman yet."

Harry heard Nathan's "yet" loud and clear. Nathan knew her, therefore he must have excluded her from consideration. Which hurt more than she had expected. "What kind of woman are you looking for?"

Nathan didn't pull any punches. "One who can stand on her own. One who can carry her half of the burden. Ranching's a hard life. I can't afford to marry a woman who can't contribute her share to making things work."

Harry threaded her hands together in her lap. Well, that settled that. She obviously wasn't the kind of

PLAY
SILHOUETTE'S

LUCKY HEARTS GAME

PLAY "LUCKY HEARTS" AND YOU COULD GET...

★ Exciting Silhouette Desire® novels—FREE
★ Victorian Picture Frame—FREE
★ Surprise mystery gift that will delight you—FREE

THEN CONTINUE YOUR LUCKY STREAK WITH A SWEETHEART OF A DEAL

When you return the postcard on the opposite page, we'll send you the books and gifts you qualify for, absolutely free! Then, you'll get 6 new Silhouette Desire® novels every month, delivered right to your door months before they're available in stores. If you decide to keep them, you'll pay only $2.47* per book—that's a savings of 28 cents off the cover price and there is no extra charge for postage and handling!

★ Free Newsletter!

You'll get our subscribers-only newsletter—an insider's look at our most popular authors and their upcoming novels.

★ Special Extras—Free!

When you join the Silhouette Reader Service™, you'll also get additional free gifts from time to time as a token of our appreciation for being a home subscriber.

FREE VICTORIAN PICTURE FRAME

This lovely Victorian pewter-finish miniature is perfect for displaying a treasured photograph. And it's yours FREE as added thanks for giving our Reader Service a try!

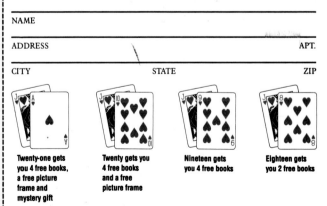
DETACH AND MAIL CARD TODAY

woman who could stand on her own two feet. In fact, Nathan had been holding her up for the past two months.

How he must have hated that! Harry thought. He had taken care of her with concern and consideration, but he had done it because she was someone who was helpless to help herself. Not as though she was an equal. Not as though she was someone who could one day be his partner. How Harry wanted the chance to show Nathan she could manage on her own! Maybe with this truce it would happen. She would continue to learn and grow. As success followed success, he would see her with new eyes. Maybe then...

Harry suddenly realized the implications of what she was thinking. She was thinking of a future that included Nathan Hazard. She pictured little Nathans and Harrys—blue-eyed blondes and brown-eyed brunettes with freckles. Oh, what a lovely picture it was!

However, a look at Nathan's stern visage wasn't encouraging. He was obviously not picturing the same idyllic scene.

In fact, Nathan was picturing something very similar. And calling himself ten times a fool for doing so. How could he even consider a life with Harry-et Alistair. The woman was a disaster waiting for a place to happen. She didn't know the first thing about ranching. She was a tenderfoot. A city girl. She would never be the kind of partner who could pull her own weight.

Fortunately they had reached the turnoff to the restaurant at Chico. The lag in the conversation wasn't as noticeable because Nathan took the opportunity to fill Harry-et in on the history of Chico. The hotel and restaurant were located at the site of a natural hot spring that now fed into a swimming pool that could be seen from the bar. It had become a hangout for all the movie stars who regularly escaped the bright lights and big city for what was still Montana wilderness. The pool was warm enough that it could be used even when the night was cool, as it was this evening.

Nathan and Harry were a little early for their dinner reservations, so Nathan escorted her into the bar where they could watch the swimmers.

"Would you like to take a dip in the pool?" Nathan asked. "They have suits—"

"Not this time," Harry said. "I don't think—" Harry stopped in midsentence, staring, unable to believe her eyes. She pointed toward the sliding glass doors. "Doesn't that man in the pool look a lot like—"

"Luke," Nathan finished for her. "I think you're right. He seems to be with someone. Maybe they'd like to join us for a drink. I'll go see."

Nathan had grasped at the presence of his friend as though it were a lifeline. He had realized, suddenly and certainly, that it wasn't a good idea to be alone with Harry-et Alistair. The more time he spent with her, the lower his resistance to her. If he wasn't careful, he'd end up letting his heart tell his head what to do. He could use his friend's presence to help him keep his sense of perspective. Of course, knowing Luke, and seeing how cozy he was with the lady, he knew his friend wasn't going to appreciate the interruption. But, hell, what were friends for?

Thus, a moment later he was standing next to Luke and the woman who had her face hidden against his chest. "Hey, Luke, I thought it was you. Who's that with you?"

After a brief pause, Luke answered, "It's Abby."

Nathan searched his memory for any woman he knew by that name. "Abby?"

"Abigail Dayton," Luke bit out.

"From Fish and Wildlife?" Nathan asked, astonished.

Abigail turned at last to face him. "Luke and I are just relaxing a few tired muscles."

Nathan grinned. "Yeah. Sure."

A female voice from the doorway called, "Nathan?"

The light behind Harry made her face nearly invisible in the shadows. At the same time it silhouetted a fantastic figure and a dynamite pair of legs. It irked Nathan that Luke couldn't seem to take his eyes off the woman in the doorway.

"Who's that with you?" Luke asked Nathan.

"Uh..."

"Nathan, is it Luke?" Harry asked. "Oh, hello. It is you. Nathan thought he recognized you."

This time it was Luke who stared, astonished. "Harry? That's Harry?"

Harry grinned. "Sure is. Nathan tried to convince me to take a swim, but I was too chicken. How's the water?" she asked Abigail.

"Marvelous."

"What are you two doing here together?" Luke asked his friend sardonically. "I thought you hated each other's guts."

Nathan stuck a hand in the trouser pocket of his western suit pants to keep from clapping it over his friend's mouth. "We called a truce. Why don't you two dry off and join us for a drink?" he invited.

Nathan could see Luke wasn't too hot on the idea. But he gave his friend his most beseeching look, and at last Luke said, "Fine."

Luke gave Nathan a penetrating stare, but made no move to leave the pool. Obviously Luke wanted a few more minutes alone with the Fish and Wildlife agent. Nathan turned to Harry-et and suggested, "Why don't we go inside and wait for Luke and Abby."

He took Harry's arm and led her back inside. "You really look beautiful tonight, Harry-et," he said as he seated her at their table.

"Thank you, Nathan." Ever since she'd come outside Nathan had been looking at her a little differently. She'd seen the admiration in Luke's eyes, and watched Nathan stiffen. Really, men could be so funny sometimes. There was no reason for Nathan to be jealous. She didn't find Luke's dark, forbidding looks nearly so attractive as she found Nathan's sharp-boned Nordic features.

She was almost amused when Nathan took her hand possessively once he was seated across from her. He held it palm up in his while his fingertips traced her work-roughened palm and the callused pads of her fingertips.

Harry felt goose bumps rise on her arm. She was all set for a romantic pronouncement when Nathan said, "It's a shame you have to work so hard. A lady like you shouldn't have calluses on her hands."

Harry jerked her hand from his grasp. "I have to work hard."

"No, you don't. Look at you, Harry-et. You spend so much time in the sun your face is as freckled as a six-year-old's."

"Are you finished insulting me?" Harry asked, confused and annoyed by Nathan's behavior.

"I think you ought to sell your place to me and get back to being the beautiful woman—"

Harry's hand came up without her really being aware it had. She slapped Nathan with the full force of the anger and betrayal she was feeling. The noise was lost in the celebration of the busy bar, but it was the only sound Harry heard above the pounding of her heart. "You never wanted a truce at all, did you, Nathan? You just wanted a chance to soften me up and make another plea to buy my land. I can't think of anything lower in this life than a lying, sneaky snake-in-the-grass Hazard!"

"Now just a minute, Harry-et. I—"

She grabbed his keys from the table where he'd set them and stood up. "I'm taking your car. You can pick it up at my place tomorrow. But I don't want to see your sorry face when you do it."

"Be reasonable, Harry-et. How am I supposed to get home?"

"You can ask your friend, Luke, to give you a ride, but I'd be pleased as punch if you have to walk."

"Harry-et—"

"Shut up and listen! You're going to have an Alistair ranching smack in the middle of your land for the rest of your life, Nathan. And you can like or lump it. I don't really care!"

Harry marched out of the bar with her head held high, but she couldn't see a blamed thing through the haze of tears in her eyes. How could she have believed that handsome devil's lies? And worse, oh, far worse, how could she still want a man who only wanted her land?

Nathan stood up to follow her, and then sat back down. That woman was so prickly, so short-tempered, and so stubborn—how on earth could he want her the way he did? It was his own fault for provoking her. But he had been frightened by his possessive feelings when Luke had admired Harry-et. So, perversely, he'd enumerated to her all the reasons why he couldn't possibly be attracted to her, and managed to drive her away in the bargain.

He had to find a way to make peace with the woman. This Hazard-Alistair feud had gone on long

enough. There had to be a happy medium somewhere, some middle ground, neither his nor hers, on
which they could meet.

Nathan made up his mind to find it.

Six

How should you behave in a Woolly West bar?
Answer: You don't have to behave in a Woolly West
bar.

Over the next three weeks Nathan thought about all
the ways he could end the Hazard-Alistair feud. And
kept coming back to the same one: *He could marry
Harry-et Alistair.* Of course, that solution raised its
own set of problems. Not the least of which was how
he was going to convince Harry-et Alistair to marry
him.

The way Nathan had it figured, marrying Harry-et
would have all kinds of benefits. First of all, once they
were married, there wouldn't be any more Alistair
land; it would all be Hazard land. Second, the feud

would necessarily come to an end, since all future Hazards would also be Alistairs. And third—and Nathan found this argument for marriage both the most and the least compelling—he would have Harry-et Alistair for his wife.

Although Nathan was undeniably attracted to Harry-et, he wasn't convinced she was the right woman for him. Except every time he thought of a lifetime spent without her, it seemed a bleak existence, indeed. So maybe he was going to have to take care of her more than he would have liked. It wasn't something he hadn't done in the past. He could handle it. He had finally admitted to himself that he was willing to pull ten times the normal load in order to spend his life with Harry-et Alistair.

Only the last time he'd driven onto her place she had met him at the end of her road with a Winchester. He'd had no choice except to leave. He hadn't figured out a way yet to get past that rifle.

Nathan was sitting at his regular booth at The Grand, aimlessly stirring his chicken noodle soup, when Slim Harley came running in looking for him.

"She's done it now!" Slim said, skidding to a stop at Nathan's booth.

"Done what?"

"Lost Cyrus's ranch for sure," Slim said.

Nathan grabbed Slim by his shirt at the throat. "Lost it how? You didn't call in her bill, did you? I told you I was good for it if you needed the cash."

"Weren't me," Slim said, trying to free Nathan's hold without success. "It's John Wilkinson at the bank. Says he can't loan her any money to pay the lease on her government land. Says she ain't a good credit risk."

"Where is she now?"

"At the bank. I just—" Slim found himself talking to thin air as Nathan shoved past him and took off out the door of The Grand, heading for the bank across the street.

When Nathan entered the bank, he saw Harry sitting in front of John Wilkinson's desk. He casually walked over to one of the tellers nearby and started filling out a deposit slip.

"But I've told you I have a trust I can access when I'm thirty," Harry was saying.

"That's still four years off."

Nathan folded the deposit slip in half and stuck it in his back pocket. He meandered over toward John's desk and said, "I couldn't help overhearing. Is there anything I can do to help, Harry-et?"

She glared at him and stared down at her hands, which were threaded tightly together in the lap of her overalls.

"So, John, what's the problem?" Nathan asked, setting a hip on the corner of the banker's oversize desk.

"Don't expect it's any secret," John said. "Mizz Alistair here doesn't have the cash to renew her government lease. And I don't think I can risk the bank's money making her a loan."

"What if I cosign the note?" Nathan asked.

"No!" Harry said, shooting to her feet to confront Nathan. "I don't want to get the money that way. I'd rather lose the ranch first!"

The banker stroked his whiskered chin with a bony hand. "Well, now, sounds like maybe we could work something out here, Mizz Alistair."

"I meant what I said," Harry declared, her chin tilting up mulishly. "I don't want your money if Nathan Hazard has to cosign the note. I'll go to a bank in Billings or Bozeman. I'll—"

"Now hold on a minute. There's no call to take your business elsewhere." John Wilkinson hadn't become president of the Big Timber First National Bank without being a good judge of human nature. What he had here was a man-woman problem, sure as wolves ate sheep. Only both the man and the woman were powerful prideful. The man wanted to help; the woman wanted to do it on her own.

"I might be willing to make that loan to you, Mizz Alistair, if Nathan here would agree to advise you on ranch management till your lamb crop got sold in the fall."

Nathan frowned. Teaching ranch management to Harry-et Alistair was a whole other can of worms from cosigning her note.

"Done," Harry said. She ignored Nathan and stuck out her hand to the banker, who shook it vigorously.

"Now wait a minute," Nathan objected. "I never said—"

"Some problem, Nathan?" the banker asked.

Nathan saw the glow of hope in Harry's eyes, and didn't have the heart to put it out. "Aw, hell, I'll do it."

"I'll expect you over later today," Harry said, throwing a quick grin in Nathan's direction. "I have a problem that needs solving right away." She turned to the banker and added, "I'll pick up that check on Monday, John."

Nathan stood with his mouth hanging open as Harry marched by him and out the door.

"That's quite a woman," the banker said as he stared after her.

"You can say that again," Nathan muttered. "She's Trouble with a capital T."

"Never saw trouble you couldn't handle," the banker said with a confident smile. "Anything else you need, Nathan?"

"No thanks, John. I think you've done quite enough for me today."

"We aim to please, Nathan. We aim to please."

Nathan was still half stunned as he walked out of the bank door and headed back to The Grand. He found Slim sitting at his booth, finishing off his chicken noodle soup.

"Didn't know you was coming back, Nathan," Slim said. "I'll have Dora Mae ladle you up another bowl."

"I'm not hungry."

"What happened?" Slim asked. "Mizz Alistair get her loan?"

"She got it," Nathan snapped. "But it's going to cost me plenty."

"You loan her the money?" Slim asked, confused.

"I loaned her *me*." Nathan sat down and dropped his head into his hands. "I'm the new manager for Cyrus's ranch."

Word spread fast in the Boulder River Valley, and by suppertime it was generally believed that Nathan Hazard must have lost his mind...or his heart. Nathan was sure it was both.

Of course, on the good side, he had Harry-et Alistair exactly where he wanted her. She would have to see him, whether she wanted to or not. He would have a chance to woo her, to convince her they ought to become man and wife. Unfortunately, he still had a job to do—making her ranch profitable—which he took seriously. And Harry-et didn't strike him as the sort of woman who was going to take well to the kind of orders he would necessarily have to give.

Meanwhile, Harry was in hog heaven. She had what she had always wanted—not someone to do it for her, but someone to teach her how to do it herself. Of course, having Nathan Hazard for her ranch manager wasn't a perfect solution. She still had to put up with the man. But once she had learned what she needed to know, she wouldn't let him set foot on her place again.

Harry was especially glad that she had secured Nathan's expertise today, because now that she had the funds to pay the lease on her mountain grazing land, she had another problem that needed to be resolved. So when Nathan arrived shortly after dark, Harry greeted him at her kitchen door with a smile of genuine welcome.

"Come in," she said, gesturing Nathan to a seat at the kitchen table. "I've got some coffee and I just baked a batch of cookies for you."

"They smell great," Nathan said, finding himself suddenly sitting at the table with a cup of coffee and a plateful of chocolate chip cookies in front of him.

Harry fussed over him like a mother hen with one chick until he had no choice except to take a sip of coffee. He had just taken his first bite of cookie, and was feeling pretty good about the way this was turning out, when Harry said, "Now, to get down to business."

With a mouthful of cookie it was difficult to protest.

"The way I see it," Harry began, "I haven't been doing all that badly on my own. All I really need, what I expect from you, is someone I can turn to when I hit a snag."

"Wait a minute," Nathan said through a mouthful of cookie he was trying desperately to swallow. "I think you're underestimating what it takes to run a marginal spread like this in the black."

"I don't think I am," Harry countered. "I'll admit I've made some mistakes, like the one I wanted to see you about tonight." Harry paused and caught her lower lip in her teeth. "I just never thought he'd do such a thing."

"*Who* would do *what* thing?" Nathan demanded.

"My shepherd. I never thought he'd take his wages and go get drunk."

"You paid your shepherd his wages? Before the summer's even begun? Whatever possessed you to do such a thing?"

"He said he needed money for food and supplies," Harry said. "How was I supposed to know—"

"Any idiot could figure out—"

"Maybe an idiot could, but I'm quite intelligent myself. So it never occurred to me!" Harry finished.

"Aw, hell." Nathan slumped back into the chair he hadn't been aware he'd jumped out of.

Harry remained standing across from him, not relaxing an inch.

"So what do you want me to do?" Nathan asked when he thought he could speak without shouting.

"I want you to go down to Whitey's Bar in Big Timber and get him out, then sober him up so he can go to work for me."

"I don't think this is what John Wilkinson had in mind when he suggested I manage your ranch," Nathan said, rubbing a hand across his forehead.

"I would have gone and done it myself if I'd known you were going to make such a big deal out of it," Harry muttered.

Suddenly Nathan was on his feet again. "You stay out of Whitey's. That's no place for a woman."

"I'm not just a woman. I'm a rancher. And I'll go where I have to go."

"Not to Whitey's, you won't."

"Oh, yeah?" she goaded. "Who's going to stop me?"

"I am."

Harry found herself in Nathan's grasp so quickly that she didn't have a chance to escape. She stared up into his blue eyes and saw he'd made up his mind she wasn't going anywhere. She hadn't intended to force a confrontation, yet that was exactly what she'd done. She didn't want Nathan doing things *for* her; she wanted him doing things *with* her. So she made herself relax in his hold, and even put her hands on his upper arms and let them rest there.

"All right," she said. "I won't go there alone. But I ought to be perfectly safe if I go there with you."

"Harry-et—"

"Please, Nathan." Nathan's hands had relaxed their hold on her shoulders, and when Harry stepped closer, they curved around her into an embrace. Her hands slid up to his shoulders and behind his neck. He seemed a little unsure of what she intended. Which was understandable, since Harry wasn't sure what she intended herself—other than persuading Nathan to make her a partner rather than a mere petitioner. "I really want to help," she said, her big brown eyes locked on Nathan's.

"But you—"

She put her fingertips on his lips to quiet him, then rested one hand against his chest, so she could feel the heavy beat of his heart, while she let the other drift up to play with the hair at his nape. "This is important to me, Nathan. Let me help."

Harry felt Nathan's body tense beneath her touch, and thought for sure he was going to say no. A second later she was sure he was going to kiss her.

She was wrong on both counts.

Nathan determinedly put his hands back on her shoulders and separated them by a good foot. Then he looked her right in the eye. "Just stay behind me and let me do the talking."

"You've got a deal! When are we going?"

A long-suffering sigh slipped through Nathan's lips. "I suppose there's no time like the present. If we can get your shepherd dried out, we can move those sheep up into the mountains over the weekend."

Whitey's Bar in Big Timber was about what you would expect a Western bar to be: rough, tough and no holds barred. It was a relic from the past, with everything from bat-wing doors to a twenty-foot-long bar with brass rail at the foot, sawdust on the floor and a well-used spittoon in the corner. The room was thick with cigarette smoke—no filter tips to be found here—and raucous with the wail of fiddles from a country tune playing on the old jukebox in the corner.

Some serious whiskey-drinking hombres sat at the small wooden tables scattered around the room. Harry was amazed that both cowboys and sheepmen caroused in the same bar, but Nathan explained that they relished the opportunity to argue the merits of their particular calling, with the inevitable brawl allowing them all an opportunity to vent the violence that civilization forced them to keep under control the rest of the time.

"Is there a fight every night?" Harry asked as they edged along the wall of the bar, hunting for her shepherd.

"Every night I've been here," he answered.

Harry gave him a sideways look, wondering how often that was. But her attention was distracted by what was happening on the stairs. Two men were arguing over a woman. Nathan hadn't exactly been honest when he'd said no women ever went to Whitey's. There were women here, all right, but they were working in an age-old profession. Twice in the few minutes they'd been in the bar, Harry had seen a woman head upstairs with a man.

The argument over the female at the foot of the stairs was escalating, and Harry noticed for the first time that one man appeared to be a cowboy, the other a sheepman.

Then she spotted her shepherd. "There he is!" she said to Nathan, pointing at a white-bearded old man slumped at a table not too far from the stairs.

Nathan swore under his breath. In order to get to the shepherd, he had to get past the two men at the foot of the stairs. He turned to Harry-et. "Wait for me outside."

Harry started to object, but the fierce look in Nathan's eyes brooked no refusal. Reluctantly she turned and edged back along the wall toward the door. She never made it.

"Why, hello there, little lady. What brings you here tonight?"

The cowboy had put one hand, which held a beer bottle, up along the wall to stop her. When she turned to face him, he braced his palm on the other side of her, effectively trapping her.

"I was just leaving," Harry said, trying to duck under his arm.

He grabbed her sleeve, and she heard a seam rip as he pushed her back against the wall. "Not so fast, darlin'."

Harry's eyes darted toward Nathan. He had just slipped his hands under the drunken shepherd's arms and was lifting him out of his chair. She couldn't bear the thought of shouting for help, drawing the attention of everyone in the bar. So she tried again to handle the cowboy by herself. "Look," she said, "I just came here to find someone—"

"Hell, little lady, you found me. Here I am."

Before Harry realized what he was going to do, the cowboy had pressed the full length of his body against her to hold her to the wall and sought her mouth with his.

She jerked her face from side to side to avoid his slobbering kisses. "Stop! Don't! I—"

An instant later the cowboy was decorating the floor and Nathan was standing beside her, eyes dark, nostrils flared, a vision of outrage. "The lady doesn't care for your attentions," he said to the burly cowboy. "I suggest you find someone who does."

The cowboy dragged himself up off the ground, still holding the neck of the beer bottle, which had broken off when he'd fallen. He recognized Nathan for a sheepman, which magnified the insult to his dignity. With all eyes on him there was no way he could back down. "Find your own woman," he blustered. "I saw her first."

"Nathan, please, don't start anything," Harry begged.

Nathan took his eyes off the other man for a second to glance at Harry, and the cowboy charged.

"Nathan!" Harry screamed.

Nathan's hand came up to stop the downward arc of the hand holding the broken bottle, while his fist found the cowboy's gut. The cowboy bent over double, and Nathan straightened him with a fist to the chin. The man crumpled to the floor, out cold.

Nathan looked up to find that pandemonium had broken out in the bar. He grabbed Harry's wrist. "Let's get out of here."

"Not without my shepherd!"

"Are you crazy, woman? There's a fight going on."

"I'm not leaving without my shepherd!"

Nathan dodged a flying chair to reach the drunken man he'd left sitting against the wall. He picked the man up, threw him over his shoulder fireman-style and marched back through the melee to Harry. "Are you satisfied?"

Harry grinned. "Now I am."

Nathan grabbed her wrist with his free hand, and glaring at anyone foolish enough to get in his way, was soon standing outside in front of Whitey's. He dumped the shepherd none too gently into the back of his pickup and ordered Harry to get in.

She hurried to obey him.

Nathan took out his fury at Harry-et on the truck, gunning the engine, only to have to slam on the brakes when he caught the red light at the corner. He raced the engine several times and made the tires squeal when he took off as the light turned green.

"Did that bastard hurt you?" he demanded through tight lips.

"I'm all right," Harry said soothingly. "I'm fine, Nathan. Nothing happened."

"You had no business being there in the first place. You should have stayed home where you belong."

"I had as much right to be there as you. More right," she argued. "It was my shepherd we went after."

"You and your damned shepherd. The greenest greenhorn would know not to pay the man in advance. This whole business tonight was your fault."

"I didn't do anything!" Harry protested.

"You were there. That was enough. If I hadn't been there—"

"But you were," Harry said. "And you were wonderful."

That shut him up. How could you complain when a woman was calling you wonderful? But if anything had happened to her... Nathan had known his feelings toward Harry-et were possessive, but he hadn't known until tonight that she was *his woman*. Woe be unto the man who harmed the tiniest hair on her head.

Nathan shook his head in disbelief. He hadn't been involved in one of Whitey's barroom brawls since he'd been a very brash young man. If this evening was any indication of what he had in store as the manager of Cyrus's ranch, he had a long, long summer ahead of him.

As they pulled up in front of Cyrus's cabin, Harry said, "If you'll leave my shepherd in the sheep barn, I'll do what I can to sober him up."

"I'll take him home with me," Nathan countered. "I'm sure my housekeeper has some Blackfoot remedy that'll do the trick. We'll be back here bright and early tomorrow morning. Think you can stay in a western saddle long enough to help us drive your sheep into the mountains?''

"I rode hunters and jumpers in Virginia."

Nathan shook his head in disgust. "I should have known. All right. I'll be here at dawn. Be ready."

Harry stepped down out of the truck and started toward the house. An instant later she ran back around the truck and gestured for Nathan to open his window.

"I just wanted to thank you again." She leaned over and kissed him flush on the mouth. "You were really wonderful." Then she turned and ran into the cabin.

Nathan waited until he saw the lights go on before he gunned the engine and took off down the rutted road. Before he'd gone very far he reached up to touch his lips where she'd kissed him. There was still a bit of dampness there, and he touched it with his tongue. And tasted her. His lips turned up in a smile.

He felt as if he could move mountains.

He felt as if he could soar in the sky.

He felt like a damn fool in love.

He felt really wonderful.

Seven

When Wade or Clyde or Harley comes a-courtin', how will you, the greenhorn female person, recognize a compliment?
Answer: He'll compare your hair to the mane on his sorrel horse.

Harry had aches where she'd forgotten she had muscles. She knew how to ride, but that didn't mean she'd done much riding lately. Her back, thighs and buttocks could attest to that. But she had accomplished what she'd set out that morning to do. Her flock of sheep had been moved up into the leased mountain pastures, and the wiry old shepherd had been settled in his gypsy wagon with a stern warning to keep a sharp eye out for wolves.

Harry was doing the same thing herself. Actually, she was keeping a sharp eye out for one particular wolf. Nathan Hazard had been acting strangely all day. Silent. Predatory. He hadn't done anything overtly aggressive. In fact, he seemed to be playing some sort of game, stalking her, waiting for the moment when he could make his move. Her nerves were beginning to fray.

After the fracas of the previous evening, Harry hadn't expected Nathan to be enthusiastic about joining her on this mountain pilgrimage. Nor was he. But at least he hadn't said a word about what had happened in Whitey's Bar. Of course, he hadn't said much of anything. Harry had been determined not to provoke him in any way, so she had kept her aches and pains to herself. Was it any wonder she had leaped at Nathan's suggestion that they halt their trek halfway down the mountain and take a rest? She had to bite her lip to keep from groaning aloud when she dismounted, but she was so stiff and sore that her knees nearly buckled when she put her weight on them.

Nathan heard Harry's gasp and turned to watch her grab the horn of the saddle and hang on for a few moments until her legs were firmly under her. He had to hand it to the woman. She was determined. He couldn't help admiring her gumption. Nathan had suspected for some time that Harry was feeling the effects of the long ride. That had suited him just fine. He'd had plans of his own that depended on getting her off that horse while they were still in the mountains. They had reached Nyla's Meadow. The time had come.

He spread a family heirloom quilt in the cool shade of some jack pines and straightened the edges over the layer of rich grass that graced the mountain meadow. At the last moment he rescued a handful of flowers that were about to be crushed, bringing them to Harry.

"Here. Thought you might like these."

Harry smiled and reached out a hand for the delicate blossoms. She brought them to her nose and was surprised at the pungent sweetness of the colorful bouquet. "They smell wonderful."

"Thought you also might like to lie down for a while here on Nyla's Meadow," Nathan said nonchalantly, gesturing toward the inviting square of material.

Harry wasted no time sagging down onto the quilt. She groaned again, but it was a sound of satisfaction as she stretched out flat on her back. "You have no idea how good this feels."

He settled himself Indian-style on a corner of the quilt near her head. "Don't guess I do. But if you moan any louder some moose is going to come courting."

Harry laughed. "I'll try to keep it down." She turned on her side and braced her head on her elbow, surveying the grassy, flower-laden clearing among the pines and junipers. "Nyla's Meadow. That sounds so beautiful. Almost poetical. How did this place get its name?"

Nathan's lips twisted wryly. "It's a pretty far-fetched story, but if you'd like to hear it—"

"Yes, I would!" Harry tried sitting up, but groaned and lay back down. "Guess I've stiffened up a little." She massaged the nape of her neck. "Make that a lot."

"I'd be glad to give your shoulders a rubdown."

That sounded awfully good to Harry. "Would you?"

"Sure. Turn over on your stomach."

A moment later Nathan was straddling her at the waist and his powerful hands had found the knots in her shoulders and were working magic. "You have no idea how good that feels," she said with another groan of pleasure.

Nathan's lips curled into a satisfied smile. Oh, yes, he did. He longed for the time when there would be nothing between his fingertips and her skin. And it seemed like he'd been waiting his whole life for this woman. He didn't plan to wait much longer.

Harry felt the strength in Nathan's hands, yet his touch was a caress. A frisson of excitement ran the length of her spine. She imagined her naked body molded to Nathan's. Joined to Nathan's. Harry closed her eyes against the vivid picture she'd painted. She had no business thinking such thoughts. The sheep-man only wanted her land. He'd as much as told her she wasn't the woman for him. And last night certainly couldn't have convinced him she would be the kind of wife he had in mind. No, the minute she had learned all she could from him, she intended to bid him a fast farewell.

So why was her body coming alive to his touch? Why did she yearn for his hands to slip around and cup her breasts, to mold her waist and stroke the taut and achy places that had nothing to do with the long ride of the morning? Harry tensed against the unwelcome, uncontrollable sensations deep inside.

"Relax," Nathan murmured as his hands slipped down from her shoulders to the small of her back and began to massage the soreness away.

"Tell me about Nyla's Meadow," Harry said breathlessly.

Nathan's thumbs slowly worked their way up her spine, easing, soothing, relaxing. "Nyla was an Egyptian princess."

Harry lifted herself on her hands and turned to eye Nathan over her shoulder. "What?"

Nathan shoved her back down. "Actually, the princess's name was N-I-L-A, after the Nile River, but somewhere over the years the spelling got changed."

"How did a Montana meadow get named after an Egyptian princess?" Harry asked suspiciously.

"Be quiet and listen and I'll tell you. Long before the first settlers came to the Boulder River Valley, a mountain man named Joshua Simmons arrived here. He had traveled the world over just for the pleasure of seeing a new horizon, or so the story goes. He'd been to Egypt and to China and to the South Sea islands. But when he reached Montana, he knew he'd found

God's country—limitless blue skies, snowcapped mountains and grassy prairies as far as the eye could see."

"You're making this up, aren't you?" Harry demanded.

"Shut up and listen," Nathan insisted. His hands moved down Harry's back to her waist and around to her ribs, where they skimmed the fullness of her breasts at the sides before moving back to her spine.

Harry shivered. She would have asked Nathan to stop what he was doing, but his hands were there and gone before she could speak. The sensations remained. And the ache grew.

"When Joshua reached this meadow, he encountered an Indian maiden," Nathan continued. "She appeared as exotic to him, as foreign and mystical, as an Egyptian princess."

"The Princess Nila," Harry murmured sardonically.

"Right. They fell in love at first sight. And made love that same day here on the meadow. When he awoke, the Indian maiden—though she was a maiden no more—was gone. Joshua never learned her name, and he never saw her again. But he never forgot her. He named this place Nyla's Meadow after the Egyptian princess she had reminded him of."

Harry shifted abruptly so that her buttocks rocked against Nathan. He felt his loins tighten and rose slightly to put some space between the heat of their two bodies.

Oblivious to Nathan's difficulties, Harry rolled over between his legs and scooted far enough away to sit up facing him. He was still straddling her at thigh level. "So Nyla's Meadow is a place for falling in love? A place where lovers meet?" she teased. She pulled the band off one braid and began to unravel it, seemingly unconscious of the effect her action would have on Nathan.

Nathan swallowed hard. "Yes. A place for lovers." He couldn't take his eyes off Harry-et. Her gaze was lambent, her pupils dilated, her lids lowered. She was clearly aroused, yet her mood seemed almost playful, as though she didn't realize the powerful need she had unleashed within him.

When Harry started to free her other braid, Nathan reached out a hand. "I'll do that."

Her hands dropped onto his thighs. And slid upward.

Nathan hissed in a breath and put his hands over hers to keep them from moving any farther. There was no need for her to actually touch him. The mere thought of her hands on him excited him. He slid her hands back down his thighs, away from the part of him that desperately wanted her touch. When he was relatively sure he'd made his position clear, he let her hands go and reached for the other braid.

Her hair was soft, and rippled where the tight braids had left their mark. When both braids were unraveled, he thrust his hands into her rich brown hair and spread the silky mass around her head and shoulders like a nimbus. "You are so beautiful, Harry-et."

Harry hadn't meant to let the game go so far. She hadn't realized just how aroused Nathan was. She hadn't realized how the sight of his desire would increase her own. Now she wanted to see what would happen next. Now she wanted to feel what she had always imagined she would feel in a lover's embrace. Her hands once again followed the corded muscles along Nathan's thighs until she reached the part of him that strained against the worn denim. She molded the shape of him with her hands, awed by the heat and hardness of him.

Nathan closed his eyes and bit the inside of his mouth to keep from groaning aloud. The sweetness of it. The agony and the ecstasy of it. "Harry-et," he gasped. "Do you know what you're doing?"

"No," she replied. "But I'm learning fast."

Choked laughter erupted from Nathan's throat. At the same time he grabbed her by her wrists and lowered her to the ground, pinning her hands above either side of her head. He stretched out over the length of her, placing his hips in the cradle of her thighs. "That's what you're doing, lady," he said in a guttural voice, thrusting once with his hips. "I want you, Harry-et."

Harry heard the slight hesitation between the two syllables as he spoke her name that made the word an endearment. He wanted her, but he hadn't spoken of needing, or caring. Maybe that was as it should be.

Alistairs and Hazards were never meant to love. History was against it. She wanted him, too. Wasn't that enough?

The decision was made for her when Nathan captured both her wrists in one hand and reached down between the two of them to caress the heart of her with the other. She felt herself arching toward him, toward the new and unbelievable sensations of pleasure.

Nathan caught her cries of ecstasy with his mouth. His kisses were urgent, needful. He let go of her wrists because he needed his hand to touch her, to caress her. When he did, Harry's fingers thrust into Nathan's hair and tugged to keep him close, so she could kiss him back. Her hands slipped down to caress his chest through his shirt, but the cotton was in her way. She yanked on his shirt and the snaps came free. She quickly helped him peel the shirt down off his shoulders. Just as quickly he freed the buttons of her shirt and stripped it off, along with her bra.

An instant later they paused and stared at each other.

Harry had seen Nathan's muscular chest once before and wanted to touch. Now she indulged that need. Her fingertips traced the crease down the center of his chest to his washboard belly.

He had imagined her naked a dozen, dozen times, but still had failed to see her as beautiful as she was. Her breasts were full and the nipples a rose color that drew his eye, his callused fingers and finally his mouth.

Harry's fingernails drew crescents on Nathan's shoulders as his mouth and tongue suckled her breast. She arched toward him, urging him to take more of her into his mouth. He cupped her breast with his hand and let his mouth surround her, while his teeth and tongue turned her nipple into a hard bud.

Harry moaned. Her body arched into his, her softness seeking his hardness.

"Please." She didn't know what came next. She'd always stopped in the past before she got this far. Only this time she didn't want to stop. She wanted to know how it ended.

"It's all right, sweetheart," he murmured in her ear. "Soon. Soon."

"Now, Nathan. Now."

He sat up and pulled off her boots, and then began pulling his own off. They both rid themselves of their jeans in record time. Nathan threw his jeans aside, then went searching for them a moment later. He ransacked the pockets, cursing as he went.

"Did you forget something?" Harry asked.

Nathan grinned as his fisted hand withdrew from his jeans pocket. "Nope."

Suddenly Harry was aware of her nakedness. And Nathan's. He looked awfully big. Not that she had anything to compare him with, but surely that thing was too large to fit . . .

"What's the matter, Harry-et?" Nathan said as he lay down beside her and pulled her into his embrace.

"Nothing," she mumbled against his chest.

"Having second thoughts?" Nathan held his breath, wondering why he was giving her a chance to back away when he wanted her so much that he was hurting.

Harry had opened her mouth to suggest maybe this wasn't such a good idea when Nathan's lips closed over hers. His tongue traced the edges of her mouth and then slipped inside, warm and wet. Seducing. Entrancing. Changing her mind all over again.

"Hold this for me," he said. "I need both hands free."

"What is it?" she asked through a haze of euphoria.

He quickly removed the foil packet and dropped a condom into her palm.

"Oh. Dear. Oh." Harry giggled with embarrassment. In her nervousness Harry was unable to keep from blurting something she'd read in a magazine article. "It's Mr. Prophylactic. The guy with the cute little button nose."

Nathan burst out laughing.

Harry blushed a fiery red. Thank goodness Nathan still had his sense of humor. Maybe this wasn't going to be so impossible, after all. Her relief was premature.

"Would you like to put it on me?" he asked.

"I've never done it before," she admitted. "I wouldn't know how. I might do it wrong."

A frown arose between Nathan's brows. He couldn't believe she'd be so irresponsible as not to use some kind of protection in this day and age. As Harry's eyes fell, the truth dawned on Nathan. *She hadn't used protection because she hadn't needed it.*

"How long?" he demanded, grasping her hair and angling her face up toward him.

"What?"

"How long since you've been with a man."

"I haven't ever... that is... this is the first time."

Nathan watched as she lowered her eyes to avoid his gaze, as if she'd committed some kind of crime. Didn't she know what a precious gift she was giving him? Didn't she know how special she had made him feel? He pulled her into his arms and held her tightly. He had never felt so protective of a woman in his life. He was awed to be the man she had chosen. And terrified by the responsibility she had placed in his hands.

"The first time for a woman... sometimes there's pain," he said, his mouth close to her temple. "I don't want to hurt you, sweetheart."

"You won't," Harry reassured him.

"Darling, sweetheart, I wouldn't mean to, but I'm afraid—"

Harry pushed him far enough away that she could see his face. "You? Afraid? Of what?"

He looked her in the eye. "That it won't be everything you expect. That it won't be perfect."

Harry smiled a beatific smile. "If I'm with you, Nathan, it will be perfect. Trust me."

He eased her back down on the quilt and lowered himself beside her, giving her a quick, hard hug.

Harry noticed something different about the embrace. Something missing. She chanced a brief glance down at him. "Oh, no," she said, dismayed.

"What's the matter Harry-et?"

"You're not . . . well, you're not . . . anymore," she said, pointing at a no-longer-aroused Nathan.

Nathan chuckled. "You're precious, Harry-et," he said with a quick grin. "One of a kind."

Harry took a swipe at his shoulder with her fist—the same fist that was still holding the condom he'd handed to her. "I don't like being laughed at, Nathan."

He laughed. "I'm not laughing at you." He rolled over onto his back and let his arms flop free, a silly grin on his face.

Harry tackled him.

An instant later she was under him, his body mantling hers. His mouth found hers, and he kissed her with all the passion he felt for her. His hands found her breasts and teased the nipples to a peak. He felt the blood thrumming through the veins in her throat with his mouth. By the time his hand finally slipped between their bodies, she was wet.

And he was hard.

"Oh. It's back," she said in an awed voice.

Nathan grinned. "So it is. Where is Mr. Prophylactic?"

Harry grinned and opened her hand to reveal a slightly squashed condom. "Will it still work?"

"Not unless you put it on."

Her chin slipped down to her chest. She glanced up at him shyly. "Will you help me?"

Nathan helped her place the condom and roll it on until he was fully covered. The way she handled him so carefully, as though he would break, made him feel treasured and very, very special.

"Is that all there is to it?" she asked.

"Pretty simple, huh?"

She caressed him through the sheath. "Can you still feel that?"

Nathan jerked. "Uh-huh."

"Really?" She let her fingers trace the shape of him, encircle him, run down the length of him from base to tip. "You can feel that?"

Nathan inhaled sharply. Slowly he inserted a finger inside her. "Can you feel that?"

Harry gasped. "Uh-huh."

He inserted another finger. "And that?"

Harry tightened her thighs around his hand, reminding Nathan this was new to her. He slowly worked his fingers inside her, stretching her, feeling the tightness and the wetness. He had to be patient. And gentle. And exercise rigid control over a body that ached with wanting her.

"Harry-et," he breathed against her throat. "Touch me."

Harry had been too caught up in her own sensations to think about Nathan's. Until he'd spoken she hadn't been aware that her hands each grasped a handful of quilt. She brought her hands up to grasp his waist instead. Slowly her fingers slipped around to his belly and down to the crease where hip met thigh.

Nathan grunted. The feel of her fingertips on his skin, on his belly, in those other places he hadn't known were so sensitive, was exquisite.

Harry relaxed her thighs, allowing Nathan greater freedom of movement. His mouth found a breast and teased it, then moved down her ribs to her belly, and then lower, where it replaced his hands at the portal she had guarded against invasion for so many years.

Her hands clutched his hair as she arched up toward the sensations of his mouth on her flesh. "Nathan, please," she cried. She had no idea what it was she needed, but she was desperate.

Nathan's eyes glittered with passion as he rose over her. She expected one quick thrust, and was prepared for the pain. Instead she felt the tip of him pushing against her. Just when she started to feel the pain, he distracted her by nipping her breast. Then his mouth found hers and his tongue mimed the action below. Thrusting and withdrawing. Pushing farther each time. Teasing and tempting. A guttural sound rose in her throat as she surged toward him, urging him inside.

Nathan thrust once more with tongue and hips, and filled her full.

Harry tensed with the extraordinary feeling of being joined to Nathan. Her legs captured his hips and held him in thrall. As he withdrew and thrust again, she met his rhythm, feeling the tension build within. His hand came between them to touch her and intensify the need for relief. For release. For something.

Harry was gasping for air, her heart pounding, her pulse racing. "Nathan," she cried. "Please. I ache. Make it stop."

God, he loved her! He wanted to say the words. Here. Now. But once said, they couldn't be taken back. He had no idea how she felt about him. She trusted him; that much was clear. But did her feelings for him run as deep as his for her? She hadn't offered those three words; there was no way he could ask for them. He could only show her how he felt, and trust that it would be enough.

"Come with me, sweetheart. Let yourself fly. It's all right. I'll take care of you."

Harry took him at his word and let herself soar. Nathan joined her in her aerie, two souls surpassing the physical, seeking a world somewhere beyond Nyla's Meadow.

It was long moments later before either of them touched ground again. Their bodies were slick with sweat, despite the shade in which they lay. Nathan was stretched out beside her with an arm and a leg thrown possessively over her. He couldn't see Harry's face, so he wasn't able to judge what she was thinking. But there was a tension in her body that was at odds with the release he'd felt within her just moments before.

"Harry-et? What's wrong?" He must have hurt her. He hadn't meant to, but he had.

She sighed. A huge, deafening sound. Those last few words Nathan had spoken before she had found ecstasy resounded in her ears: "I'll take care of you." Those words reminded her of why it would be foolish to give her heart to Nathan Hazard. She wanted to stand on her own two feet. He was liable to sweep her off them. She freed herself from his embrace and sat up, pulling her knees to her chest and hugging them with her arms. "This can't happen again, Nathan."

"I'm sorry if I hurt you. I—"

"You didn't hurt me, Nathan. I just don't want to do it . . . this . . . with you again."

"It sounds to me like you're sorry it happened the first time," he said angrily, sitting up to face her. "You were willing. You can't deny it."

"I'm not denying it. I wanted this as much as you," she admitted. "I'm only saying it can't happen again."

"Give me one good reason why not," he demanded.

Because I'm in danger of falling in love with you.

Because I'm in danger of losing myself to you.

Because I find you irresistible, even though I know we have no business being together like this.

That was three reasons. None of which she had any intention of mentioning to him. Harry turned away from him and slipped on her bra and panties. She could hear the rustle of clothing behind her as he dressed. The metal rasp of the zipper on his jeans was loud in the silence. She stood and pulled up the zipper on her own jeans before reaching for her boots.

He grabbed the boot out of her hand and shook it, then handed it back to her. "Snakes," he said curtly. "And spiders."

Harry shivered and made sure she dumped the other boot as well before she slipped it on. His warning had been an abrupt reminder that she was a very sore tenderfoot. Harry couldn't very well avoid Nathan until she learned everything from him that she needed to know. She would just have to learn to control the need to touch, and be touched, that arose every time she got near him.

Nathan had no idea what he'd done that was so wrong, but after the most profound lovemaking he'd ever experienced, Harry-et was avoiding him as if he had the measles. She wasn't going to get away with it.

"Harry-et."

"Yes, Nathan?"

"Come here."

"No." Harry turned and marched over to the tree where her horse was tied. She tried to mount, but couldn't raise her leg high enough to reach the stirrup. She laid her face against the saddle and let her shoulders slump.

An instant later Nathan grabbed her by the waist and hoisted her into the saddle. "Move your leg out of the way, tenderfoot," he ordered.

Harry gritted her teeth and did as he ordered, painfully sliding her leg up out of his way as he worked on the saddle.

"Damned good thing you couldn't reach the stirrup," he snarled. "Damn cinch wasn't tightened. Saddle would have slid around and dumped you flat."

"Stop treating me like I'm helpless!" she snapped. "I can take care of myself."

"I'll believe it when I see it," he retorted.

"I pulled my own weight today. Don't tell me I didn't."

Nathan neither confirmed nor denied her assertion. He tightened the cinch on his own saddle and mounted, then reined his horse to face her. "That story I told you about Nyla's Meadow?"

"Yes?"

"I made it all up."

Harry struggled to keep the disappointment out of her voice. "All of it?"

"Every last word. No one knows how the meadow got its name."

He had invented a place for falling in love. A place where lovers meet. Then brought her here. And made love to her. Now he wanted her to believe it had all been a lie.

"We made love in Nyla's Meadow, Nathan. That was real."

Nathan met her imploring gaze with stony eyes. "We had sex. Damn good sex. But that's all it was." And if she believed that, he had a bog he'd like to sell her for grazing land.

He was waiting for the retort he was sure was on her lips. But she didn't argue, just kicked her horse and loped away from him toward the trail back down the mountain.

"Damn you, Harry-et!" he muttered. "Damn you for stealing my heart and leaving *me* feeling helpless."

He kicked his horse and loped down the mountain after her. As he followed her down the mountain, he thought back on the day he'd spent working with Harry-et. Not once had she asked for his help. Not once had she complained. In fact, she had done extraordinarily well for a tenderfoot. Was it possible that someday Harry-et Alistair could actually stand on her own two feet? He found the idea fascinating if far-fetched. He stared at the way she rode stiff-backed in the saddle. She had grit, that woman. It sure couldn't hurt to hang around long enough to find out!

Harry's thoughts weren't nearly so sanguine. All day she had been careful not to let Nathan do too much. If she was going to feel like a success, she had to make it on her own. She had left her family to get away from people ordering her around. But somehow Nathan had never ordered her to do anything. He had made suggestions and left the decisions up to her. So maybe she could endure his company a little longer. Maybe she could forget what had happened between them today in Nyla's Meadow and simply take advantage of his expertise.

But it was clear she was going to have to be careful. Give Nathan an inch and he might take an acre. And the man had made no secret of the fact that he wanted the whole darn spread.

Eight

In a small town out West what do you do if you become ill?
Answer: Put on a big pot of coffee, because an hour after you get your prescription from the drugstore, five people will phone with sympathy and two will fetch you a hot dish.

Harry didn't see Nathan for a week, but he called her every day with instructions for some job or other that she had to complete: repairing the henhouse, planting a vegetable garden, spreading manure, harrowing the fields and cleaning the sheep shed. She took great pride in the fact that she managed to accomplish every task alone. Successfully. She knew Nathan had expected her to cave in and ask for help long before now. So when he phoned one evening and told her to clean out all the clogged irrigation channels on her property in preparation for starting the irrigation water through the main ditch, she headed out bright and early the next morning, expecting to get the job done. And failed abysmally.

All Harry could figure was that Nathan had left something out of his instructions. She tried calling him for more directions, but he was out working in his fields and couldn't be reached until noon. She left a message with Nathan's housekeeper for him to call her as soon as he got in.

Nathan did better than that. Shortly after noon he arrived on her kitchen doorstep. ''Harry-et, are you in there? Are you all right?''

He didn't wait for her to answer, just shoved the screen door open and stepped inside. When Nathan saw her sitting at the table with a sandwich in her hand, his relief was palpable. His heart had been in his throat ever since he'd read the message Katoya had left him. He'd had visions of Harry wounded and bleeding from some farm accident. He was irritated that he cared enough about her to feel so relieved that she wasn't hurt. He forced the emotion he was feeling from his voice and asked, ''What was the big emergency?''

''No emergency,'' Harry answered through a mouthful of peanut butter and jelly. ''I just couldn't get the irrigation system to work with the directions you gave me.''

"What was wrong with my directions?"

"If I knew that, I wouldn't have called you."

"I'll go take a look."

"I'll come with you." She threw her sandwich down and headed toward him.

Nathan felt his groin tighten at the sight of Harry sucking a drop of grape jelly off her finger. "Don't bother. I can do it quicker on my own."

Harry hurried to block his exit from the kitchen. "But if I don't come along, I won't know what I did wrong the next time I have to do it by myself," she pointed out in a deceptively calm voice.

Nathan stared at the jutting chin of the woman standing before him. Stubborn. As a mule. And sexy. Even in bibbed overalls. "All right," he muttered. "But don't get in my way."

When Nathan crossed behind the barn, he saw the backhoe sitting in the middle of her field by the main irrigation ditch. "I didn't know you could manage a backhoe." Handling the heavy farm machinery was how he'd feared she'd hurt herself.

"It wasn't so hard to figure out. I used it to widen the main ditch and clear the larger debris from the irrigation channels. But I still didn't get any water."

She was a remarkable woman, all right. It wasn't the first time he'd had that thought, but Nathan didn't understand why it irritated him so much to admit it now. Could it be that he *wanted* her to need him? *Needed* her to need him? What if she turned out to be really self-sufficient? Where did that leave him? *With an Alistair smack in the middle of his property.* Nathan pursed his lips. The thought didn't irk him near as much as it ought to.

When they arrived at the main ditch, Nathan examined her work. He could find no fault with it. "Did you follow the main ditch all the way across your property?"

"As far as that stand of cottonwoods over there along the river." She didn't add that the thought of snakes hiding in the thick vegetation around the cottonwoods had scared her off.

"Let's go take a look."

Harry was happy to follow him. The way Nathan was stomping around it wasn't likely any snake was going to hang around long enough to take him on.

Harry stayed close behind Nathan and actually bumped into him when he stopped dead and said, "There's your problem."

She leaned around him to see where he was pointing. "That bunch of sticks?"

"Beaver dam. Has to come out of there. It's blocking the flow of water along the main ditch."

"How do I get rid of it?"

Nathan grinned ruefully. "Stick by stick. You'd better head back to the house and get your thigh-high rubber boots."

"Rubber boots? Thigh-high?"

"I take it you don't have any rubber boots," Nathan said flatly.

"Just my galoshes."

He sighed. "They're better than nothing. Go put them on. Get a pair of gloves, too."

"All right. But don't start without me," she warned.

"Wouldn't think of it."

Harry ran all the way to the cabin, stepped into her galoshes and galomphed all the way back to the beaver dam. True to his word, Nathan was sitting on a log that stuck out from the dam, doing nothing more strenuous than chewing on a blade of sweet grass. But he hadn't been idle in her absence. He was leaning on two shovels, wore thigh-high rubber boots and had a pair of leather gloves stuck in his belt.

"All ready?" he asked.

"Ready."

The beaver dam was several feet long and equally wide and thick, and Harry felt as if she were playing a game of Pick-up Sticks. She never knew whether the twig she pulled would release another twig or tumble a log. Leaves and moss also had to be shoveled away from the elaborate dam. The work was tedious and backbreaking. Toward the end of the afternoon it looked as if they might be able to clear the ditch before the sun went down, if they kept working without a break.

Harry was determined not to quit before Nathan. Sweat soaked her shirt and dripped from her nose and chin. Her face was daubed with mud. Her hands were raw beneath the soaked leather gloves. There were blisters on her heels where the galoshes rubbed as she mucked her way through the mud and slime. It was little consolation to her that Nathan didn't look much better.

He had taken off his shirt, and his skin glistened with sweat. He kept a red scarf in the back pocket of his jeans, and every so often he pulled it out and swiped at his face and neck and chest. Sometimes he missed a spot, and she had the urge to take the kerchief from his hand and do the job for him. But it was as plain as peach pie cooling on a windowsill that Nathan was a heap better at dishing out help than he was at taking it. And though they worked side by side all day, he kept his distance.

Touching might be off-limits, but that didn't mean she couldn't look. Harry was mesmerized by the play of corded muscles under Nathan's skin as he hefted logs and shoveled mud. She turned abruptly when he caught her watching, and was thankful for the mud that hid her flush of chagrin.

Nathan hadn't been as unaware of Harry as he'd wanted her to think. The outline of her hips appeared in those baggy overalls every time she stretched to reach another part of the dam. He had even caught a glimpse of her breasts once when she'd bent over to help him free a log. There was nothing the least bit attractive about what she had on. He didn't understand why he couldn't seem to take his eyes off her.

Suddenly, as though they'd opened a lever, the water began to rush past them into the main irrigation ditch and outward along each of the ragged channels that crisscrossed Harry's fields.

"It's clear! We did it!" Harry shouted, exuberantly throwing her arms into the air and leaping up and down.

Nathan saw the moment she started to fall. One of her galoshes was stuck in the mud, and when Harry started to jump, one foot was held firmly to the ground while the other left it.

Nathan was never quite sure later how it all happened. He made a leap over some debris in an attempt to catch Harry-et before she fell, but tripped as he took off. Thus, when he caught her, they were both on their way down. He twisted his body to take the brunt of the fall, only his boot was caught on something and his ankle twisted instead of coming free. They both hit the ground with a resounding "Ooomph!"

Neither moved for several seconds.

Then Harry untangled herself from the pile of arms and legs and came up on her knees beside Nathan, who still hadn't moved. "Nathan? Are you all right? Say something."

Nathan said a four-letter word.

"Are you hurt?"

Nathan said another four-letter word.

"You *are* hurt," Harry deduced. "Don't move. Let me see if anything's broken."

"My shoulder landed on a rock," he said between clenched teeth as he tried to rise. "Probably just bruised. And my ankle got twisted."

"Don't move!" Harry ordered. "Let me check."

"Harry-et, I—" He sucked in a breath of air as he sat up. His right shoulder was more than bruised. Something was broken. "Help me up."

"I don't think—"

"Help...me...up," he said through gritted teeth.

Harry reached an arm around him and tried lifting his right arm to her shoulder. He grunted.

"Try the other side," he told her.

She slipped his other arm over her shoulder and used the strength in her legs to maneuver them both upright.

Nathan tried putting weight on his left leg. It crumpled under him. "Help me get to that boulder over there."

Harry supported Nathan as best she could, and with a sort of hopping, hobbling movement that left him gasping, they made it. She settled Nathan on the knee-high stone and stood back, facing him with her hands on her hips. "I'll go get the pickup. You need a doctor."

"I'll be fine. Just give me a minute to rest." A moment later he tried to stand on his own. The pain forced him back down.

"Are you going to admit you need some help? Or do I have to leave you sitting here for the next few weeks until somebody notices you're missing?"

"Go get the pickup," he snarled.

"Why thank you, Mr. Hazard, for that most brilliant suggestion. I wish I'd thought of it myself." She sashayed away, hips swaying. Her attempt at nonchalance was a sham. As soon as she was out of sight, she started running, and sprinted all the way to her cabin. She tore through the kitchen, hunting for the truck keys, then remembered she'd left them in the ignition. She headed the pickup straight back across the fields, skidding the last ten feet to a stop in front of Nathan.

"You just took out half a field of hay," Nathan said.

"I'm afraid I was in too much of a hurry to notice," she retorted. She forced herself to slow down and be gentle with Nathan as she helped him into the truck, but even so, the tightness of his jaw, and his silence, attested to his pain.

"Where's the closest hospital?" she demanded as she scooted behind the wheel.

"Take me home."

"Nathan, you need—"

"Take me home. Or let me out and I'll walk there myself."

"You need a doctor."

"I'll call Doc Witley when I get home."

It didn't occur to her to ask whether Doc Witley practiced on humans. It shouldn't have surprised her that he turned out to be the local vet.

Several hired hands came running when Harry drove into Nathan's yard, honking her horn like crazy. They helped her get Nathan upstairs to the loft bedroom of his A-frame home. Harry's mouth kept dropping open as she took in her surroundings. She had never suspected Nathan's home would be so beautiful.

The pine logs of which the house was constructed had been left as natural as the day they were cut. The spacious living room was decorated in pale earth tones, accented with navy. A tan corduroy couch and chair faced a central copper-hooded fireplace. Nearby stood an ancient wooden rocker. The living room had a cathedral ceiling, with large windows all around, so that no matter where you looked there was a breathtaking view: the sparkling Boulder River bounded by cottonwoods to the east; the Crazy Mountains to the north; the snowcapped Absarokas to the south; and to the east, pasture land dotted with ewes and their twin lambs.

If this was an example of how Nathan Hazard designed homes, the world had truly lost someone special when he had given up his dream.

If she'd had any doubt at all about his eye for beauty, the art and artifacts on display in his home laid them fully to rest. Bronze sculptures and oil and watercolor paintings by famous western artists graced his living room. Harry indulged her curiosity by carefully examining each and every one during the time Doc Witley spent with Nathan.

When the vet finally came downstairs, he found Harry waiting for him.

"How is he?"

"Nothing's broke."

"Thank God."

"Dislocated his shoulder, though. Put that to rights. Couldn't do much with his ankle. Bad sprain. May have cracked the bone. Can't tell without an X ray and don't think he'll hold still for one. Best medicine for that boy is rest. Keep him off his feet and don't let him use that shoulder for a few weeks. I'll be going now. Have a prize heifer calving over at the Truman place. You mind my words now. Keep that boy down." He gave her a bottle of pills. "Give him a couple of these every four hours if he's in pain."

Harry looked down to find the vet had handed her a bottle of aspirin. She showed him out the door and turned to stare up toward the loft bedroom that could be seen from the living room. Nathan must have heard what the doctor had said. It shouldn't be too hard to get him to cooperate. For the first time since she'd arrived, Harry realized Nathan's housekeeper hadn't made an appearance. Maybe Katoya was out shopping. If so, Harry would have to stick around until she got back. Nathan was in no shape to be left alone.

Nathan's bedroom was done in darker colors: rust, burnt sienna and black. The four-poster bed was huge, and flanked by a tall, equally old-fashioned piece of furniture that Harry assumed must hold his clothes. The other side of the room was taken up by a rolltop desk. The oak floor was mantled with a bearskin rug. Of course there were windows, wide, clear windows that brought the sky and the mountains inside.

Nathan had pillows piled behind his shoulders and an equally large number under his left foot.

She took a step into his bedroom. "Is there anything I can do for you?"

"Just leave me alone. I'll manage fine."

"Your home is lovely. You show a lot of promise as an architect," she said with a halting smile.

"It turned out all right," he said. "As soon as it was built, I thought of a dozen things I could have done better."

She didn't feel comfortable encroaching farther into his bedroom, so she leaned back against the doorway. "You'll make all those improvements next time."

"A sheepman doesn't have the leisure time to be designing houses," he said brusquely.

"Actually, you're going to have quite a bit of free time over the next couple of weeks," she replied. "The vet gave orders for you to stay in bed. By the way, I haven't seen your housekeeper. Do you expect her back soon?"

"In about a month," Nathan said. "She left early this afternoon to visit her granddaughter, Sage Littlewolf, on the Blackfoot reservation up near Great Falls."

"Do you suppose she'd come back if she knew—"

"Yes, she would. Which is why I have no intention of contacting her. There's some problem with her granddaughter that needs settling. She's gone there to settle it. I'll manage."

Harry marched over to stand at Nathan's bedside. "How do you intend to get along without any help?"

"It's not your problem."

"I'm making it my problem."

"Look, Harry-et, I don't need your help—"

"You need help," she interrupted. "You can't walk."

"I'll use crutches."

"With your right arm in a sling?"

"I'll hop."

"What if you fall?"

"I won't."

"But if you do—"

"I'll get back up. I don't need you here, Harry-et. I don't want you here. I don't think I can say it any plainer than that."

"I'm staying. Put that in your pipe and smoke it, Mr. Hazard." Harry turned and headed for the door.

"Harry-et, come back here! Harry-et!"

She kept on marching all the way downstairs until she stood in his immaculate, perfectly antiquated kitchen, trying to decide what she should make for his supper.

Nathan spent the first few minutes after Harry left the room, proving he could get to the bathroom on his own. With his father's cane in his left hand he was able to hobble a little. But it was an awkward and painful trip, to say the least. He couldn't imagine trying to get up and down the stairs to feed himself. Of course, he could sleep downstairs on the couch, but that would put the closest bathroom too far away for comfort.

By the time Harry showed up with a bowl of chicken noodle soup on a wicker lap tray, Nathan was willing to concede that he needed someone to bring his meals. But only for a day or so until he could get up and and down stairs more easily.

"All right, Harry-et," he said, "you win. I'll send a man to take care of your place for the next couple of days so you can play nursemaid."

"Thank you for admitting you need help. I, on the other hand, can manage just fine on my own."

"Look, Harry-et, be reasonable. There's no sense exhausting yourself trying to handle two things at once."

"I *like* exhausting myself," Harry said contrarily. "I feel like I've accomplished something. And I'm quite good at managing three or four things at once, if you want to know the truth."

"Stop being stubborn and let me help."

"That's the pot calling the kettle black," she retorted.

"Have it your way, then," he said sullenly.

"Thank you. I will. I'll be back in a little while to collect your soup bowl. Be sure it's empty." She stopped on her way out the door and added, "I'll be sleeping on the couch downstairs. That way you can call if you need me during the night."

Nathan was lying back with his eyes closed when Harry returned for the dinner tray he had set aside. She sat down carefully beside him on the bed, so as not to wake him. He was breathing evenly, and since she believed him to be asleep, she risked checking his forehead to see if he had a fever. Just as she was brushing a lock of blond hair out of the way, his eyes blinked open. She saw the pain before he thought to hide it from her.

She finished her motion, letting it be the caress it had started out as when she'd thought he was asleep. "I was checking to see if you have a fever."

"I don't."

"You do."

He didn't argue. Which was all the proof she needed that he wasn't a hundred percent. "Doc Witley left some aspirin. He said you might need it for the pain. Do you?"

"No."

She sighed. "I'll leave two on the bedside table with a glass of water, just in case."

He grabbed her wrist as she was rising from the bed to keep her from leaving. "Harry-et."

"What is it, Nathan?"

The words stuck in his throat, but at last he got them out. "Thank you."

"You're welcome, Nathan. I—"

Harry was interrupted by a commotion downstairs. "What on earth—" Someone was coming up, taking the stairs two at a time.

"Hey, Nathan," a masculine voice shouted, "heard you slipped and landed flat on your ass—" Luke stopped abruptly when he saw Harry Alistair standing beside Nathan. "Sorry about the language, ma'am." He tipped his hat in apology. "Didn't know there were ladies present."

"How on earth did you find out what happened?" Harry asked. "I swear I haven't been near a phone—"

"No phone is as fast as gossip in the West," Luke said with a grin. "I'm here to see if there's anything I can do to help out."

Nathan opened his mouth to respond and then closed it again, staring pointedly at Harry.

"I was just taking this downstairs," she said, grabbing Nathan's dinner tray. "I'll leave you two alone." She hurried from Nathan's bedroom, closing the door behind her.

Luke turned back to Nathan and waggled his eyebrows. "Should have known you wouldn't spend your time in bed all alone."

"Watch what you say, Luke," Nathan warned. "You're talking about a lady."

"So that's the way the wind blows."

"Harry-et is only here as a nurse."

"One of the hired hands could nurse you," Luke pointed out.

"She refuses to leave, so she might as well do some good while she's here," Nathan said defensively.

"Who's going to take care of her place while she's taking care of you?"

Nathan grimaced. "I offered to have one of my hands help her out. She insists on doing everything herself. Look, Luke, I'd appreciate it if you'd look in on her over the next couple of days. Make sure she doesn't overdo it."

"Sure, Nathan. I'd be glad to."

"I'd really appreciate it. You see, Harry-et just doesn't know when to quit."

"Sounds a lot like my Abby."

"Your Abby?"

"Abigail Dayton and I got engaged yesterday."

"I thought you hadn't seen her since she caught that renegade wolf and headed back home to Helena."

"Well, I hadn't. Until yesterday. I figured life is too short to live it without the woman you love. I was already headed over here to give you the big news when I heard about your accident."

Nathan reached out and grasped Luke's hand. "I really envy you. When's the wedding?"

Luke grinned wryly. "As soon as my best man is back on his feet again. You'd better make it quick, because Abby's pregnant."

Harry heard Nathan's whoop at the same time she heard the front door knocker. She didn't know which one to check out first. Since the door was closer, she hurried to open it.

"Hi! I'm Hattie Mumford. You must be Harry Alistair. I'm pleased to meet you. I brought one of my apple spice cakes for Nathan. Thought it might cheer him up. Can I see him?''

The door knocker rattled again.

"Oh, you get the door, dear," Hattie said. "I know the way upstairs."

Harry just barely resisted the urge to race up ahead of Hattie to warn Nathan what was coming. The knocker rapped again. She waited to answer it because Luke was skipping down the stairs.

"Is he all right?" Harry asked anxiously. "I heard him holler."

Luke grinned. "Nathan was just celebrating the news of my engagement and forthcoming marriage to Abigail Dayton."

"You and Abigail?" Harry smiled. "How wonderful! Congratulations!"

"You'd better get that door," Luke said. "I'll just let myself out the back way."

Harry opened the door to a middle-aged couple.

"I'm Babs Sinclair and this is my husband, Harve. We just heard the bad news about Nathan. Thought he might enjoy my macaroni-and-cheese casserole. I'll just take this into the kitchen. Harve, why don't you go up and check on Nathan."

For want of something better to do, Harry followed Babs Sinclair into the kitchen. The woman slipped the casserole into the oven and turned on the heat. Harry didn't have the heart to tell her Nathan had already eaten his supper.

"You better get some coffee on the stove, young'un," Babs said. "If I know my Harve, he'll—"

"Babs," a voice shouted down from the loft, "send some coffee up here, will you?"

The door knocker rapped.

"You better get that, young'un. I'll take care of making the coffee."

For the next three hours neighbors dropped by to leave tokens of their concern for Nathan Hazard. Besides the apple spice cake and the macaroni-and-cheese casserole, Nathan had been gifted with a loaf of homemade bread and a crock of newly made butter, magazines, and a deck of cards. The game of checkers was only on loan and had to be returned once Nathan was well. Harry met more people that evening than in the nearly four months since she'd moved to the Boulder River Valley.

What she hadn't realized until Hattie Mumford mentioned it was that her neighbors had been waiting for her to indicate that she was ready for company. They would never have thought to intrude on her solitude without an invitation. Now that Harry was acquainted with her neighbors, Hattie assured her they would all make it a point to come calling.

Over the next few weeks as she nursed Nathan, Harry was blessed with innumerable visits from the sheepmen of Sweet Grass County and their wives. They always turned up when she was busy with chores and managed to stay long enough to see them finished. She found herself the recipient of one of Hattie's apple spice cakes. And she thoroughly enjoyed Babs Sinclair's macaroni-and-cheese casserole.

It never occurred to her, not once in all the propitious visits when she'd been exhausted and a neighbor had arrived to provide succor, that while she had been acting as Nathan's hostess in the kitchen, he had been upstairs entreating, encouraging and exhorting his friends and neighbors to keep an eye out for her while he was confined to his bed.

So when Harry overheard Hattie and Babs talking about how she was a lucky woman to have Nathan Hazard *taking care of her,* she began asking a few questions.

When Nathan woke up the next morning and stretched with the sunrise, he yelped in surprise at the sight that greeted him at the foot of his bed.

Nine

How do you know when a handsome Woolly West-
erner is really becoming dead serious about you?
Answer: He invites you to his ranch and shows you a
basket overflowing with three hundred unmated socks.
You realize your own heart is lost when you begin
pairing them.

Nathan wasn't a good patient. He simply had no experience in the role. He was used to being the caretaker. He didn't know how to let somebody take care
of him. Harry bore the brunt of his irascibility. Well,
that wasn't exactly true. Nathan had more than once
provoked an argument and found himself shouting at
thin air. Over the three weeks he'd spent recuperat-
ing, he'd learned that Harry picked her fights.

So when he woke up to find her standing at the foot of his bed, fists on hips, brown eyes flashing, jaw clamped tight to still a quivering chin, he knew he was in trouble.

"I have tried to be understanding," she said hoarsely. "But this time you've gone too far."

"I haven't left this bed for three weeks!" he protested.

"You know what I mean! I found out what you did, Nathan. There's no sense trying to pretend you didn't do it."

Nathan stared at her, completely nonplussed. "If I had the vaguest idea what you're talking about, Harry-et—"

"I'm talking about what you said to Hattie Mumford and Babs and Harve Sinclair and Luke Granger and all the other neighbors who've been showing up at my place over the past three weeks to *help* me. How could you?" she cried. "How could you?"

Harry turned her back to him and walked over to the window to look out at the mountains. "I thought you understood how important it was to me to manage on my own," she said in an agonized voice.

She swiped the tears away, then turned back to face him. "Do you know how many times over the past three weeks I've let you do something for yourself, knowing it was more than you could handle? Sometimes you surprised me and managed on your own. More often you needed my help. But I never offered it until you asked, Nathan. I respected your right to decide for yourself just how much you could handle.

"That's all I ever wanted, Nathan. The same respect I was willing to give to you." Her lips curled as she spit out, "Equal partners. You have no concept what that means. Until you do, you're going to have a hard time finding a woman to *share* your life."

As she whirled and fled the room, Nathan shouted, "Harry-et! Wait!" He shoved the covers out of the way and hit the floor with both feet.

Harry was halfway down the stairs when she heard him fall. She paused, waiting for the muttered curse that would mean he was all right. When it didn't come, she turned and ran back up the stairs as fast as she could. He was lying facedown on the bearskin rug, his right arm hugged tightly to his body. She fell onto her knees beside him, her hands racing over him, checking the pulse at his throat. "Nathan. Oh, God. Please be all right. I—"

An instant later he grasped her wrist and pulled her down beside him. A moment after that he had her under him and was using the weight of his body to hold her down. "Stop bucking like that," he rasped. "You're liable to throw my shoulder out again."

"You'll be lucky if that's all the damage I do," she snapped back at him. She shoved at his chest with both hands, and knew she'd hurt him when his lips drew back over his teeth.

"That's it." He caught both of her hands in one of his and clamped them to the floor above her head.

With his other hand he captured her chin and made her look at him. "Are you going to listen to me, or not?"

"I don't know anything you could say—"

"Shut up and let me talk!"

She pressed her lips into a flat, uncompromising line and glared at him.

"I want another chance," he began. She opened her mouth, and he silenced her with a hard kiss. "Uh-uh," he said, wagging a finger at her. "Don't interrupt, or I'll have to kiss you again."

She narrowed her eyes, but said nothing.

"I've listened to every word you've ever said to me since I met you, but I never really heard what you were saying. Until just now. I'm sorry, Harry-et. You'll never know how sorry. I guess the truth is, I didn't want you to be able to manage on your own."

"Why not?" she cried.

He swallowed hard. "I wanted you to need me." He paused. "I wanted you to love me."

"Oh, Nathan. I do. I—"

He kissed her hard to shut her up so that he could finish, but somehow her lips softened under his. Her tongue found the seam of his lips and slipped inside and searched so gently, so sweetly, that he groaned and returned the favor. It was a long time before he came to his senses.

"So, will you give me another chance?" he asked.

She smiled. "Will you call off your neighbors?"

"Done. I have one more question to ask."

"I'm listening."

"Will you marry me?"

The smile faded from her lips and worry lines furrowed her brow. "I do love you, Nathan, but..."

"But you won't marry me," he finished tersely.

"Not right now. Not yet."

"When?"

"When I've proved I can manage on my own," she said simply. "And when I'm sure you've learned what it means to be an equal partner."

"But—"

She put her fingertips on his lips to silence him. "Let's not talk any more right now, Nathan. There are other things I'd rather be doing with you." She suited deed to word and let her fingers wander over his face in wonder. To the tiny crow's-feet at the corners of his eyes. To the deep slashes on either side of his mouth. To the bristled cheeks that needed shaving.

"Smile for me, Harry-et."

It was harder than she'd thought it would be. She had just turned down a proposal of marriage from a man she loved. Harry told herself she'd done the right thing. If she'd said yes, she would never have known for sure how much she could accomplish by herself. When she sold her lambs in the fall and paid off the bank, then she'd know for sure. Then, if Nathan held to his promise to treat her as an equal, she could marry him. That was certainly something she could smile about.

Nathan watched the smile begin at the corners of her mouth. Then her lower lip rounded and her upper lip curled, revealing the space between her two front teeth that he found so enchanting. He captured her mouth and searched for that enticing space with his tongue, tracing it, and then the roof of her mouth, and the soft underskin of her upper lip. Then his teeth closed gently over her lower lip and nibbled before his tongue sought the honeyed recesses of her mouth once more.

Harry groaned with pleasure. She wasn't an anxious virgin now. She knew what was coming. Her body responded to the memories of Nathan's lovemaking that had never been far from her mind over the past month since they had made love. But she saw the flash of pain when Nathan tried to raise himself on his arms. And that took away all the pleasure for her.

"Nathan. Stop. I think we should wait until your shoulder's better before—"

He rolled over onto his back and positioned her on his belly, with her legs on either side of him. "There. Now my shoulder will be fine."

"But how..."

His hands cupped her breasts through her shirt, his thumbs teasing the nipples into hard buds. "Use your imagination, sweetheart. Do whatever feels right to you."

Harry smiled. Nathan wasn't wearing a shirt. She took both of his hands and laid them beside him on the bearskin rug. "Don't move. Until I say you can."

Then she leaned over and circled his nipple with her tongue. His gasp widened her grin of delight. Her fingertips traced the faint traces of bruise that were the only remaining signs that he'd dislocated his shoulder. Her lips soothed where her fingers had been. She traced the length of his neck with kisses and nipped the lobe of his ear. Then her tongue traced the rim of his ear, and she whispered two words she'd never thought she'd say out loud to a man. She saw his pulse jump, felt his breath halt. The guttural sound in his throat was raw, filled with need.

His hands clutched her waist and pulled her hard against him, but she sat up abruptly. "You're not playing by the rules, Nathan," she chastised, placing his hands palm down on the floor. "No touching." She smiled a wanton, delicious smile and added, "Yet."

She felt his hardness growing beneath her and rubbed herself against him through his jeans.

"Harry-et," he groaned. "You're killing me. Whatever you do, just don't stop," he rasped.

Harry laughed at his nonsensical request. She reached down and cupped him with her hand, and felt his whole body tighten like a bowstring. Her exploration was gentle but thorough. By the time she was done, Nathan was arched off the floor, his lower lip clenched in his teeth.

"Have I ever told you what a gorgeous man you are, Nathan?"

"No," he gasped.

"You are. These high cheekbones." She kissed each one tenderly. "This stubborn chin." She nipped it with her teeth. "Those blue, blue eyes of yours." She closed them with her fingertips and anointed them with kisses. She moved down his body, her fingertips tracing the ridges and curves of his masculine form, her mouth following to praise without words.

With every caress Harry gave Nathan she felt herself blossom as a woman. She wanted a chance to return the pleasure he'd given her on Nyla's Meadow. She unsnapped his jeans and slowly pulled the zipper down. She started to pull his jeans off, then paused. Her hand slipped into his pockets one by one. Right front. Left front. Right rear. In the left rear pocket she found what she was looking for. "My, my," she said, holding out what she'd found. "Mr. Prophylactic."

"I don't know how that got there," Nathan protested.

"Just thank goodness it was, and shut up," Harry said with a laugh. She dropped the condom onto the bearskin nearby and finished dragging Nathan's jeans down, pulling off his briefs along with them, leaving him naked. And aroused.

She couldn't take her eyes off him. She certainly couldn't keep her hands off him. She opened the condom and sheathed him with it, taking her time, arousing him, teasing him, taunting him.

Nathan had reached his limit. He grasped Harry-et's shirt and ripped the buttons free. Her jeans didn't fare much better. He had her naked in under nine seconds and impaled her in ten. She was slick and wet and tight. "You feel so good, Harry-et. Let me love you, sweetheart."

Harry felt languorous. Her body surged against Nathan's. He put a hand between them, increasing the tension she felt as he sought out the source of her desire. When she leaned over, he captured her breast in his mouth and suckled her. Sensations assaulted her: pleasure, desire, and her body's pulsing demand for release.

"Nathan," she gasped.

His mouth found hers as his hands captured her hips. They moved together, man and woman, part and counterpart, equal to equal.

Harry clutched Nathan's waist, arching toward the precipice, reaching for the satisfaction that was just beyond her reach.

Nathan felt her tensing, felt her fight against release. "Let go, sweetheart. It's all right. Soar. Back to Nyla's Meadow, darling. We can go there together."

Then it was too late for words. She was rushing toward satisfaction. Nathan stayed with her, his face taut with the passion raging within him. She cried out, and he thrust again. A harsh sound rose from deep in his throat as he released his seed.

Harry felt the tears coming and was helpless to stop them. They stung her cheeks, hot and wet. Nathan felt them against his face and raised his head in disbelief.

"Harry-et?"

She reached a hand up to brush the golden locks from his brow. "It's all right, Nathan. I just felt so...overwhelmed for a moment."

He pulled her into his arms and held her tightly. "You have to marry me Harry-et. I love you. I want to keep you safe."

Harry buried her face in his shoulder. "I love you, Nathan, but it scares me."

"How so?"

"It's taken me a long time to get the courage to strike out on my own. I've hardly had a chance to try my wings."

"We'll learn to fly together, Harry-et."

What she couldn't explain, what she hardly understood herself, was her fear of surrendering her new-found control over her life. Nathan needed to be needed. She loved him enough to do anything she could to make him happy. That gave him a great deal of power. She simply had to find a way to accept his gestures of loving concern...and still keep the independence she was fighting so hard to achieve.

A knock on the door sent them both scrambling for their clothes.

"That'll be Luke," Nathan said as he yanked on his jeans. "I told him I wanted to talk over the plans for his bachelor party."

"Abigail's likely to be with him," Harry said as she tied her buttonless shirt in a knot. "I wanted to make sure it's all right with her to plan a combination bridal/baby shower."

They finished dressing at almost the same time, then stood grinning at each other.

"Shall we go greet our guests?" Nathan asked.

"I'm ready."

Harry fitted herself against Nathan as he slipped his arm around her shoulder for support. It took them a while to get downstairs, but Nathan had already shouted at Luke to let himself in and make himself at home. Sure enough, when they reached the living room, they found that Abigail was with him. After exchanging greetings, Nathan and Luke settled down in the living room while Harry and Abigail headed for the kitchen.

Luke waited only long enough for the two women to disappear before he asked, "Did you ask her?"

"Yep."

"So?"

"She said she'd think about it."

"For how long?"

Nathan thrust a hand through his hair in frustration. "She didn't give me a definite timetable. But at least until she sells her lambs in the fall."

"Guess that shoots the double wedding," Luke muttered.

"There's no reason why we can't go ahead and plan your wedding to Abby," Nathan said.

"We've got a few months yet before the baby comes. I'm willing to wait a while." He grinned. "I've gotten sort of attached to the idea of having a double wedding with my best friend."

Nathan smiled. "What's Abigail going to say about the delay?"

"You won't believe this, but I'm the one in a rush to get married. Abby says she won't love me any less if we never have a ceremony and get a legal piece of paper that proclaims us man and wife."

At that moment Harry was hearing approximately the same speech from Abigail's lips.

"I'm willing to wait to have a ceremony until you and Nathan can stand at the altar with us," Abigail said. "Really, Harry, I can't believe you turned him down!"

"I had no idea you and Luke were thinking about a double wedding with the two of us," Harry said as she measured the coffee into the pot.

"Well, now that you know, why not change your mind and say yes to Nathan?" Abigail said with an impish grin.

Harry pursed her lips. "I'm sorry to throw a screw in the works, but I have some very good reasons for wanting to wait."

"Fear. Fear. And fear," Abigail said.

"Do I hear the voice of experience talking?"

Abigail bowed in recognition of the dubious honor. "But of course. You're speaking to a woman who was afraid to fall in love again. Everyone I had ever cared about had died. I didn't want to face the pain of losing someone else I loved."

"But Luke is perfectly healthy!" Harry exclaimed.

"Reason has very little to do with fear. What is it you're afraid of, Harry?"

Harry poured a cup of coffee and stared into the blackness. "That I'll be swallowed up by marriage to Nathan." She turned and searched out Abigail's green eyes, looking for understanding. "I'm just learning to make demands. With Nathan it's too tempting to simply acquiesce. Does that make any sense?"

"Like I said, there's nothing rational about our fears. I know mine was very real. You just have to figure out a way to overcome it."

"I thought I was taking a big step just coming to Montana," Harry said. "Nathan's proposal strikes me as a pretty big leap into a pretty big pond."

"Come on in," Abigail said with a smile. "The water's fine."

Harry couldn't help smiling back at Abigail. She had come to Montana knowing there were battles to be fought and won. At stake now was a lifetime of happiness with Nathan. All she had to do was find the courage to deal with whatever the future brought.

There was yet another war to be fought, but on an entirely different field. Harry wanted to convince Nathan it wasn't too late to pursue the dreams he'd given up so long ago. She had already put her battle plan in motion.

While searching for some extra sheets in a linen closet, Harry had discovered Nathan's drafting table. It was in pieces, and she had spent the past few weeks finding the right place to locate it. She had finally set it up in front of the window that overlooked the majestic, snowcapped Absarokas. Surely such a view would provide the inspiration an aspiring architect needed.

She had seen Nathan eye the table when they'd come downstairs to greet Luke and Abigail. She knew that as soon as the couple left, she would have some fast talking to do. As Nathan waved a final goodbye to Luke and Abigail, Harry walked into the living room and settled herself in the rocker that Nathan usually claimed.

The instant he closed the front door, Nathan turned to Harry and demanded, "What's that doing in here?"

"I would think that's obvious. It's there so you can use it."

"I've already told you I don't have time for drawing," he said harshly.

"Not drawing, designing," she corrected. Harry watched him limp over to the table. Watched as his hand smoothed lovingly over the wooden surface. *He misses it.* That revelation was enough to convince Harry she should keep pushing. "I couldn't help thinking that all those movie stars moving into Montana are going to be needing spacious, beautiful homes. Someone has to design their mountain sanctuaries. Why not you?"

"I'm a sheep rancher, that's why." He settled into the ladder-back stool she had found in the tack room in the barn, and shifted the T square up and down along the edge of the drafting table. "Besides, when would I have time to draw?"

"Montana is blessed with a lot of long winter nights," she quipped.

He rose from the table and limped over to stand in front of her. "There are other things I'd rather be doing on a long winter night." He took her hands and pulled her out of the rocker and into his embrace. "Like holding my woman," he murmured in her ear. "Loving her good and hard."

"Sounds marvelous," she said. "Designing beautiful houses. Designing beautiful babies."

"You make it sound simple."

"It can be. Won't you give it a try?"

He hugged her hard. "Don't start me dreaming again, Harry-et. I've spent a long time learning to accept the hand fate has dealt me."

"Maybe it's time to ask for some new cards."

Nathan shook his head. "You never give up, do you? All right, Harry-et. I'll give it a try."

She gave him a quick kiss. "I'm glad."

Nathan had no explanation for why he felt so good. He'd given up all hope of designing significant buildings a long time ago. But mountain sanctuaries for movie stars? It was just whimsical enough to work. He would make sure that the structures fitted in with the environment, that they utilized the shapes and materials appropriate to the wide open Montana spaces. Maybe it wasn't such a crazy idea, after all.

He looked down into Harry-et's glowing brown eyes. He had never loved anyone as much as he loved her. "Come back upstairs with me," he urged.

"I can't. It's time for me to go home."

"Stay."

"I can't. I'll be in touch, Nathan. Goodbye."

Harry kept her chin up and her shoulders back as she walked out the door. It made no sense to be walking away from the man she loved. Maybe over the next few weeks she could get everything straightened out in her mind. Maybe she could convince herself that nothing mattered as much as loving Nathan. Not even the independence she had come to Montana to find.

Ten

Where is a western small-town wedding reception held?

Answer: The church basement if large enough, otherwise the Moose Hall.

Harry found it hard living in her dilapidated cabin again. Of course, her place was tiny and primitive and utterly unlivable in comparison to Nathan's. But she had coped with those things for months and had never minded. Now she couldn't wait to leave Cyrus's cabin each morning. Because it felt empty without Nathan in it.

Harry had spent a lot of time lately thinking about what was important to her. Nathan headed the list. Independence wasn't even running a close second.

Harry was having trouble justifying her continued refusal of the sheepman's wedding proposal. These days Harry was so self-sufficient that it was hard to remember a time when she hadn't taken care of herself. She was starting to feel foolish for insisting that Nathan wait for an answer until she sold her lambs and paid off her loan at the bank.

Everything was clarified rather quickly when she received a call from her father.

"Your mother and I will be coming for a visit in two weeks, Harriet, to check on your progress. While we're there we'd really like to see where you're living."

"My place is too small for company, Dad. I'll meet you at The Grand in Big Timber," Harry countered.

"By the way, how are you, darling?" her mother asked.

"Just fine, Mom. I've had a proposal of marriage," Harry mentioned casually. "From a rancher here."

"Oh, dear. Don't rush into anything, darling," her mother said. "Promise me you won't do anything rash before we get there."

"What did you have in mind, Mom?"

"Just don't get married, dear. Not until your father and I have a chance to look the young man over."

"Your mother is right, Harriet. Marriage is much too important a step to take without careful consideration."

"I'll keep that in mind, Dad. I've got to go now."
She couldn't help adding, "I've got to feed the chickens and slop the hogs."

Harry felt a twinge of conscience when she heard
her mother's gasp of dismay. But her father's snort of
disgust stiffened her resolve. She was proud of what
she'd accomplished since coming to the valley. If her
parents couldn't appreciate all she had done, that was
their loss. She wasn't going to apologize for what she'd
become. And she sure wasn't going to apologize for
the man she had just decided to marry.

As soon as her parents clicked off, she dialed Nathan's
ranch. She heard his phone ring once and
quickly hung up. This was too important an announcement
to make over the phone. Besides, she
hadn't seen Nathan for ten long, lonely days. She
wanted to be there, to see Nathan's face, and share her
excitement with him. The pigs and the chickens would
have to wait.

Halfway to Nathan's house, Harry realized he
would probably be working somewhere on the ranch,
out of communication with the house. To her surprise,
when she knocked on the door, he answered it.

"What are you doing home?" she asked as he ushered
her inside. "You're supposed to be out somewhere
counting sheep."

"I'm drawing," he said with a smug smile. "I've
been hired to design a house for a celebrity who's
moving to Big Timber. Very high-muckety-muck. Cost
is no object."

She heard the eagerness in his voice. And the pride and satisfaction. "Then I guess I'd better say yes before you get too famous to have anything to do with us small-time sheep ranchers. So, Nathan, the answer is yes."

"What did you say?"

"Yes, I'll marry you."

"Don't play games with me, Harry-et."

"I'm not playing games, Nathan. I said I'll marry you, and I meant it."

A moment later Harry knew why she'd come in person. Nathan dragged her into his arms and hugged her so tightly that she had to beg for air. Then his mouth found hers and they headed for Nyla's Meadow. When she came to her senses, she was lying under Nathan on the couch and her shirt was unbuttoned all the way to her waist. That didn't do him as much good as it might have, since she was wearing bibbed overalls that got in his way.

Nathan's mouth was nuzzling its way up her neck to her ear when he stopped abruptly. "I don't mean to look a gift horse in the mouth, Harry-et, but what changed your mind?"

"I had a call from my parents. They're coming to visit again."

"And?"

"They wanted to look you over. Like a side of beef. To make sure you were Grade A Prime. I thought that sort of behavior particularly inappropriate for a sheepman. So I've decided to make this decision without them."

"And in spite of them?" Nathan asked somberly. He sat up, pushing Harry-et off him, putting the distance of the couch between them. "I don't want you to marry me to prove a point to your parents. Or to yourself."

"My parents have nothing to do with my decision," Harry protested. "I thought you'd be happy."

"I was. I am. I just don't want you to have regrets later. Once we tie the knot, I expect it to be forever. No backing out. No second thoughts. I want you to be sure you're choosing to be a sheepman's wife—my wife—of your own free will."

Harry felt tears burning behind her eyes and a lump growing in her throat at Nathan's sudden hesitance. "Are you sure you haven't changed your mind?" she accused.

"I was never the one in doubt, Harry-et. I love you. I want to spend my life with you. You're the one who said you didn't want to give up your independence. Do you wonder that I question your sudden about-face?"

"What can I do to prove to you that I'm sincere?"

Nathan took a deep breath. "Introduce me to your parents as your fiancé. Let them get to know me without stuffing me down their throats. Give yourself a chance to react to their reactions. See if you still feel the same way after they've gone. If you want to marry me then, Harry-et, I'll have you at the altar so fast it'll make your head spin."

"It's a deal."

Harry-et held out her hand to seal the bargain and, like a fool, he took it. His reaction was the same today as it had been yesterday, as it would be tomorrow. A bolt of electricity shot up his arm, his heart hammered, his pulse quickened. But instead of letting her go he pulled her into his embrace, holding her close, breathing the scent of her—something stronger than My Sin…more like…Her Sheep. It was the smell of a sheepman's woman. And he loved her for it.

Harry suffered several bouts of ambivalence in the days before her parents were due to arrive.

Maybe she should have pressed Nathan to get married.

Maybe she should have left well enough alone.

Maybe she should have sold her lambs early.

Maybe she should have sold out and gone home long ago.

Harry didn't know why confronting her parents with her decision to marry Nathan should be so difficult. She only knew it was.

She arrived at The Grand on the appointed day with Nathan in tow. "I'll make the introductions," Harry said. "Just let me do the talking."

"It's all right, Harry-et. Relax. Your parents love you."

"I'll try to remember that." And then they were there and she was hugging her mother and then her father and Nathan was shaking their hands. "Where's Charlie?" she asked.

"Your mother and I decided to come alone."

That sounded ominous. "Mom, Dad, this is Nathan Hazard. Nathan, my mother and father."

"It's nice to see you again Mr. and Mrs. Alistair. Why don't we all go find a booth inside?" Nathan suggested.

Harry let him lead her to a booth and shove her in on one side. He slid in after her while her parents arranged themselves on the other side.

"So, Mr. Hazard—"

"Nathan, please."

"So, Nathan, what's this we hear about your wanting to marry our girl?" Harry's father demanded.

Harry groaned. She felt Nathan's hand grasp her thigh beneath the table. She took heart from his reassurance. Only his hand didn't stay where he'd put it. It crept up her thigh under the skirt she'd worn in hopes of putting her best foot forward with her parents. She grabbed his hand to keep it where it was and tried to pay attention to what Nathan was saying to her father.

"And you'd be amazed at what Harry's done with the place."

"What about that federal lease for grazing land, Harriet? Your banker told me the last time I was here that there isn't much chance he could make you a loan to cover it."

"We worked it out, Dad," Harry said. "I'll be selling my lambs in a couple of weeks. Barring some sort of catastrophe, I'll make enough money to pay off the bank and have some working capital left over for next year.''

''Well. That's a welcome relief, I imagine,'' Harry's mother said. ''Now about this wedding—''

''My mind is made up, Mom. You can't change it. I'm marrying Nathan. I love him. I want to spend my life with him.''

''I don't think I've ever heard you speak so forcefully, my dear,'' her mother said.

''It does appear you're determined to go through with this,'' her father said.

Harry's hand fisted around her fork. ''I am,'' Harry said. ''And I'm staying in Montana. I'm where I belong.''

''Well, then, I guess there's nothing left to do except welcome you to the family, young man.'' Harry's father held out his hand to Nathan, who grinned and let go of Harry's thigh long enough to shake her father's hand.

Harry was stunned at her parents' acquiescence. Was that all it took? Was that all she'd ever needed to do? Had she only needed to speak up for what she wanted all these years to live her life as she'd wanted and not as they'd planned? Maybe it was that simple. But until she'd come to Montana, until she had met and fallen in love with Nathan, Harry hadn't cared enough about anything to fight for it.

She sat up straighter in her seat and slipped her hand under the table to search out interesting parts of Nathan she could surreptitiously caress. His thigh was rock-hard under her hand. So were other parts of him.

The smile never left her face during the entire dinner with her parents.

When the meal was over, Harry's mother and father rose to leave. Nathan stayed seated, excusing himself and Harry. "We have a few more things to discuss before we go our separate ways, if you don't mind."

"Not at all," Harry's father said.

Her mother leaned over and whispered in her ear, "Your young man has lovely manners, dear. You must bring him to Williamsburg for a visit sometime soon. And let me know as soon as you set a date for the wedding."

Harry stood and hugged her mother across the table. "To tell you the truth, we'd really like to get married while you're here, so you can come to the wedding. It isn't going to be a large gathering. Just a simple ceremony with me and Nathan . . . and another bride and groom."

"A double wedding! My goodness. Who's the other happy couple? Have we met them?"

"You will. They're friends of mine and Nathan's," Harry said.

"At least let me help with the reception," her mother said.

"I don't know, Mom. You don't know anyone in town. How can you possibly—"

"Trust me, dear. Just say you'd like my help."

Harry grinned. "All right, Mom. I'll leave the reception in your hands."

Nathan waited only long enough for Harry's parents to leave before he grabbed her by the hand and hauled her out of the booth. "You've got some nerve, young lady," he said as he dragged her up the stairs and closed one of The Grand's bedroom doors behind them.

"What do you mean, Nathan?"

He caught her by the shoulders and inserted his thigh between her legs, pulling her forward so that she was riding him.

Harry gasped.

His mouth came down on hers with all the passion she'd aroused in him when he'd been unable to take her in his arms. "That'll teach you to play games under the table."

"I've learned my lesson, Nathan," she said with a sigh of contentment. "Teach me more."

Nathan reached over and turned the lock on the door. "Your wish is my command."

"Nathan?"

"Yes, Harry-et."

"I love you."

"I love you, too."

They didn't say anything for long moments because their mouths were otherwise pleasantly occupied.

"Nathan?" Harry murmured.

"Yes, Harry-et."

"Where do you suppose my mother will end up having the reception?"

"The Moose Hall," he said as he nuzzled her throat.

Harry laughed. "You're kidding."

"Nope. It's the only place available except for the church basement, and that's too small."

"Too small? How many people are you inviting?"

Nathan smiled and kissed her nose. "You really are a tenderfoot, Harry-et. Everyone in Sweet Grass County, of course."

Harry's eyes widened. "Will they all show up?"

"Enough of them to make your mother's reception a success. Now, if you're through asking questions, I'd like to kiss that mouth of yours."

"Your wish is my command," Harry replied.

Nathan laughed. "Don't overdo it, Harry-et. A simple 'Yes, dear' will do."

"Yes, dear," she answered with an impudent grin.

"You're mine now, Harry-et. Forever and ever."

"Yes, dear."

"We'll live happily ever after. There'll be no more feuding Hazards and Alistairs. Your land is mine, and my land is yours. It's all *ours*."

"Yes, dear."

"And there'll be lots of little Hazard-Alistairs to carry on after us."

Harry's eyes softened and she surrendered to Nathan's encompassing embrace. "Oh, yes, dear."

* * * * *

SILHOUETTE·INTIMATE·MOMENTS®

IT'S TIME TO MEET
THE MARSHALLS!

In 1986, bestselling author Kristin James wrote A VERY SPECIAL FAVOR for the Silhouette Intimate Moments line. Hero Adam Marshall quickly became a reader favorite, and ever since then, readers have been asking for the stories of his two brothers, Tag and James. At last your prayers have been answered!

In August, look for THE LETTER OF THE LAW (IM #393), James Marshall's story. If you missed youngest brother Tag's story, SALT OF THE EARTH (IM #385), you can order it by following the directions below. And, as our very special favor to you, we'll be reprinting A VERY SPECIAL FAVOR this September. Look for it in special displays wherever you buy books.

Silhouette Books®

Take 4 bestselling love stories FREE

Plus get a FREE surprise gift!

Coming Soon

Fashion A Whole New You. Win a sensual adventurous trip for two to Hawaii via American Airlines®, a brand-new Ford Explorer 4 × 4 and a $2,000 Fashion Allowance.

Plus, special free gifts* are yours to Fashion A Whole New You.

From September through November, you can take part in this exciting opportunity from Silhouette.

Watch for details in September.

* with proofs-of-purchase, plus postage and handling